The Executioness

The
Executioness

Tobias S. Buckell

SUBTERRANEAN PRESS 2011

First Edition

ISBN
978-1-59606-354-9

Subterranean Press
PO Box 190106
Burton, MI 48519

www.subterraneanpress.com

b19484495

Introduction

by Paolo Bacigalupi

WRITING IS A PRETTY lonely gig. Most of the time, we lock ourselves in our offices, huddle over our computers and cut ourselves off from the people around us so that we can create. Building a fictional world is work, and the outside world is the last thing you need intruding.

Which is fine. Except that it really does get lonely.

The first time I remember meeting Toby, it was at the World Fantasy Convention, in Madison, WI. He's got a different memory, but I've got the true one. Trust me. No, really. Trust me. I know when we first met, because it was all very shiny and new to me. WFC was the first major convention I'd ever attended, and I was in awe of all the writers and editors pooling in the bar and at the restaurants. Lots of talent and ideas and camaraderie for a new writer, and an especially heady experience for me because I live in the middle of nowhere.

A few days into the convention, I ended up sharing a table for lunch—for reasons I can't even remember now—with a bunch of other writers, and I ended up sitting next to this one guy who kept saying the most interesting things. That was Toby. Young and smart and friendly and lit up with ideas. His first book *Crystal Rain* was already out and getting good reviews, and he was working on a second, and he was full of the most amazing idea bombs. Before I really knew what was happening, we were deep in conversation, geeking out over high tech sailing ships, and hydrofoils and cars that run off compressed air... I walked away from that conversation with a head full of ammunition, knowing that I'd barely scratched the surface of the guy's intellect. That's Toby. Ideas layered inside of ideas layered inside of ideas. And an enthusiasm for sharing and riffing that makes him the ideal antidote to the loneliness of the writer's life.

Fast forward a couple years. Toby and I know each other a lot better, and Toby is still the guy with all the awesome ideas—I actually wrote my novel *Ship Breaker* partly based on conversations that we'd had, and even named a cannon after him in the book (if you're going to pay homage to someone, it's best done with firepower, right?) So anyway, we were driving up to the Blue Heaven writers workshop, and we were talking about the need to stay fresh with our writing, to stretch ourselves, to write new things and to keep an aspect of play in our work. With deadlines and novels under contract, it's sometimes hard to feel like you're stretching. And when you're not stretching as a writer, you're dying.

Toby mentioned a project he was fleshing out for Audible.com, a chance for him to stretch his writing chops in some new directions and to play with characters that he hadn't tried before. He had this intriguing story fragment he was working with, full of resonance and possibility, the story of a middle-aged mother who becomes a legend.

Much as I was inspired by Toby to create *Ship Breaker*, Toby had been inspired by something Maureen McHugh had said once, wondering why there were no middle-aged women cast as heroes (the cool thing about hanging out with lots of writers is that we all end up challenging and inspiring each other, and we all benefit from that exchange). In this case, Maureen wondered why women just like herself, found everywhere, extraordinary in many ways, but never particularly attended to by media or storytellers, never got top billing, and were instead ignored in favor of the next young hot thing.

Her observations got Toby thinking, and he decided to take up the challenge. To add to it, he decided to write fantasy. Both of us have our backgrounds pretty firmly grounded in science fiction, and so exploring a fantasy world appealed to him as both a place to play creatively, and to stretch into something new and unfamiliar.

To be honest, the idea appealed to me, too, and I remember wishing there was some way for me to play along. I was actually quite jealous of his project.

And then he asked if I might be interested in joining him.

He proposed a joint world, built together, with a story by each of us set in the land that we created. Did I want in? he asked.

A chance to work with someone who throws out ideas the way a machine gun spits out bullets? The chance to write fantasy? To do something totally different, and for once, not be alone in the creative process? Did I want in? Hell yeah, I wanted in.

Over the next few months, Toby and I skyped back and forth, me in Colorado, him in Ohio, using the science-fictional wonders of videoconferencing and Google Wave to create a fantasy. With the structure of his story as the backbone, we added flesh until the world came to life. We discovered Khaim and Turis, arquebusses and poisonous bramble, raiders and mayors and majisters, the Three faces of Mara, and Dog-headed Kemaz. And lying in ruins to the East, the fallen empire of Jhandpara.

It wasn't work. It was play. A big adrenaline rush of idea trading, bargaining and reimagining, as we took each other's ideas and built on them and handed them back to be built on again. That shared process meant that you had more than just what you brought to the table. It almost seemed as if you had more to work with than even both of you brought to the table—it was a hybrid, more interesting and stranger and more fun because of it. We each got to build on each other, but we also got to push each other, riffing on each other's ideas, one-upping each other, and hunting for a world that we could both agree was cool enough to set our stories in.

Working with Toby was the most fun I've had writing in a long time. It's a rush to have a partner in crime, and it's pleasure now to introduce you to *The Executioness* and her world. Enjoy.

Part One

L ET ME YOU TELL about the first time I killed a man.

On the morning of that day my father, Anto, lay on the simple, straw-stuffed mattress that I'd dragged out to the kitchen fire, choking on his own life as a wasting sickness ate at him from the inside.

He had been like this for days now. I had watched him grow thin, watched him cough blood, and listened to him swear at the gods in a steady mumble which I struggled to hear over the crackle of the kitchen fire.

I burned the fire to keep him warm, even though winters in Lesser Khaim were not the kind that kill men, like the ones far to the North. Winter was a cool kiss here, in Lesser Khaim, and the fire kept him comfortable and happy in his last days.

"Why haven't you fetched the healer yet, you useless creature," Anto hissed at me.

"Because there are none to fetch," I said firmly, gathering my skirts around my knees to crouch by his side. I put a scarred hand, the sign of my long years of slaughtering animals at the back of the butcher's shop, to his forehead. It felt hot to my old, callused palms.

There had been a healer, once. A wrinkled old man who lanced boils and prescribed poultices. But he'd been chased away by the Jolly Mayor and his city guards, accused of using magic. The old man had been lucky to flee into the forest with his life.

"Then bring someone who can *cure* me," Anto begged. "Even if they are of the deadly art. I'm in so much pain."

His pleading tore at me. I leaned closer to him and to the crackle of the fire that burned wood we could barely afford in these times, when refugees from Alacan crammed themselves into Lesser Khaim, eating and using everything they could get their hands on.

I sighed as I stood, my knees cracking with the pain of the movement. "Would you have me look for someone who can cast a spell for you, and then condemn us all to death if that's found out? It would be a heavy irony for anyone in this family to die at the blade of an executioner's axe, don't you think?"

I thought, for a moment, that he considered this. But when I looked closely at his face for a reaction, I realized he'd sunk back into his fever.

He was back to muttering imprecations at the gods in his sleep. A husk of a blasphemer, who took so much joy in seeing the pious void their bowels at the sight of his executioner's axe. This was the man who would lean close and whisper at the condemned through his mask, "Do you not believe you will visit the halls of the gods soon? Don't you burn favors for a god, perhaps one like Tuva, so that you will eat honey and milk from bowls that never empty, and watch and laugh at the struggles of mortals shown on the mirrors all throughout Tuva's hall? Or do you fear that this is truly your last moment of life?"

That was my father, the profane.

Unlike his outwardly pious victims, Anto believed. He had to believe. He was an executioner. If there were no gods, then what horrible thing was it that he did?

Now he was going to find out.

It angered him that it was taking so long to slowly waste away into death. So he cursed the gods. Especially the six-armed Borzai, who would choose which hall Anto would spend eternity in.

He swore at Borzai, even though he would soon meet the god. And even though that god would decide my father's afterlife. Anto was not the sort of man who cared. He had no thoughts for the future, and he dwelled little on the past.

I always had admired that about my father.

My oldest son, Duram, peeked around a post to look into the kitchen, his dark curly hair falling down over his brown eyes. "Is he sleeping?"

I nodded. "Are you hungry?"

"I am," Duram said. "So is Set, but he doesn't want to come down the stairs. He says it hurts."

Set had been born with a twisted foot.

"Stay quiet," I cautioned as I picked up a wooden platter. I spooned olives from a jar, tore off several large pieces of bread, cut some goat's cheese, and then lined the edges with figs.

Duram dutifully snuck back up the crude wooden stairs, and I heard the planks overhead creak as he took food to his brother. Soon he would need to work for the family. He'd need to become a man early, to help replace Anto's earnings.

But for now, I sheltered him in the attic with his brother and their toys. I wanted them both to have some peace before their worlds got harder. Particularly Set's.

I opened a window and looked outside. My husband Jorda was supposed to be working the field. Instead he was sprawled under a gnarled tree, a wineskin lying over a blistered forearm.

There was always a wineskin. I never passed him a single copper earned from my butchering, but he still found wine. He usually begged them from his friends among the Alacan refugees. He'd sit with them and loudly damn the collapse of Alacan, and they'd cheer him and buy him cheap wine.

With a sigh, I shut the wooden window.

Anto groaned and swore in his sleep, disturbed by the cold air. I would have liked to have had a healer here. Someone who could give us bitter medicine, and hope. A kind ear for the betrayals of the body.

But for all that I may have hated the Jolly Mayor for banishing the healer, my family's lives had depended on the mayor over the years. My life, my two sons, my husband, and my father. For Anto, skinny, frail, over-tempered bastard and profaner that he was, was an executioner for Khaim and the mayor.

We would have starved a long time ago without that money. The coin tossed in the executioner's cup by the soon-to-be-beheaded in hopes of buying a good cut. The coppers tossed into the bucket by the crowd. The mayor's retainer.

So when the tiny bell by the door rang, it was with the authority of a thunderclap. The tiny note floated around the old stone house, dripping into the kitchen, and wrapping itself around me as its quivering tones faded.

This was the first time it had rung since Anto had fallen sick.

He was being summoned, as executioner, to bring his axe to the square by the highest of noon.

SOMEWHERE, ACROSS the inky, shoving waters of the Sulong river, which split Lesser Khaim and Khaim, up on Malvia Hill and in Mayors House, someone had rung the executioner's bell.

The bell was magic, of course. The Mayor swore that the spells that had been cast to create the bells had been formed a long time ago, and that the bells were safe. I wondered if that was true, as I could smell magic softly in the air by the doorway whenever the bell rang. It tasted of ancient inks, herbs, and spices, and it settled deep in the back of my throat.

Once the executioner's bell was rung in Mayor House, the goddess of a thousand multiple roads and choices, Deka, dictated which executioner's bell rang back in sympathy. And Deka had chosen ours.

Deka was well known for her tricks. The goddess of dice throwers was playing one last little one on Anto.

I looked back over my thick, wooden kitchen table toward Anto. His brown eyes were wide, his brows crinkled in intense thought.

He rubbed his anemic mustache, which was a sign of his failure: that he had only ever had one child, and a daughter at that.

"The call..." he said, voice breaking. "Tana. Did you hear it?"

I moved to him. "You can't go. You know that."

I wondered, as I said it, where the gentleness in my voice had come from. It had never been offered to me in my life by this old man. Not in all the years I'd cooked and chopped wood, or the long years I'd worked as a butcher.

"I know I can't go you stupid girl," Anto spat. "It is well beyond me."

The bell here needed to be rung if an executioner were here. In five minutes, if there was no reply, the call would go to someone else.

In a way, that dying ring would signal the death of our family. Without Anto's occasional income, we would have to sell the small house and the land. And then we would become little better than the refugees around us.

I watched him lie back down into the bed, gazing up at the thick ceiling beams. "Where is Jorda?" Anto asked.

"Sleeping," I said.

"Drunk," Anto spat. "Useless. Addled."

I had nothing to say to that.

Anto's jaw set, and he said, "I have always answered the call. Always come back with the Mayor's coin to keep us alive as the bramble creeps into our useless field. I'll slit my own throat right here and now before I hand over the executioner's bell. It is all that keeps my miserable bloodline flowing."

"What are you talking about?" I asked.

Anto coughed. "The gods hate me. Had I a son, he'd be on his way right now instead of bothering me with this."

My voice jumped in anger. "Well, I'm not your son. I'm your daughter. You must live with that." And then I added, "with what little life you do have left."

Anto nodded. "This is true. This is true."

And then he crawled out of his bed. The blankets slipped off to reveal his liver-spotted arms.

"What are you doing?" I asked.

He stumbled out of the kitchen to the door, stick-like legs quivering from the effort.

I realized what he was about to do and moved to stop it, but with a last wily burst of energy, Anto staggered forward and rang the executioner's bell before I grabbed his arm.

As the single, clear note rang out and filled the back of my throat with the faint taste of old magic, he crumpled to the floor in a heap of bones and skin, laughing at me.

"Now you *have* to go in my place, little daughter of mine. Now you have no choice." He panted where he lay, staring up at me with eyes sunk deep into wasted, skeletal sockets. "The Mayor would execute both of us if you try to tell him what we just did. He is not a forgiving man."

"When you face Borzai in the Hall of Judgment, he will banish you to Zakia's torture cells for eternity," I told him. "When I hear your spirit groan in the night, tortured by dark gods, I will laugh and pretend I didn't hear it."

He flinched at that. "Do you hate me so?"

I trembled with outrage. "You bring me nothing but pain and drudgery and burden."

He thought on that for a long while. Longer than I'd seen him consider anything. "You must go just this once, then. After this, you can turn the bell in. I'll be dead soon, I can't stop you, yet you must at least cover the expense of my funeral. I'll not have my appearance in Borzai's Hall of Judgment delayed because the rites were not pleasing to him. And after that if you wish it, it could be your trade. It is a good living, daughter. And with me gone, there will be one less body to care for, one less mouth to feed. You have no field, and butchering people will give you more than butchering pigs."

Then he sighed and crawled toward his bed. I said nothing. I helped him back to it, his body surprisingly light as I slung his arm over my neck.

"How can I kill someone who has done nothing to me?" I asked.

Anto grunted. "Don't look into their eyes. Consider that the Mayor has a reason for their death. Remember that if they have led a proper life, they will be sent to the right hall for eternity."

"Won't the Mayor's guards be able to tell I'm not you?"

"No," Anto murmured. "I've been wasting away long enough. I'm a small figure, so are you. Wear my hood, carry my axe, none will be able to tell the difference. It is no different than chopping wood. Raise the axe, let it fall, don't swing it, and aim the edge for the neck. You've killed enough pigs, you can do this."

And with that, he slipped away to his sleep, exhausted by all his recent efforts.

I understood he'd always wanted a son. That he'd wanted the farm to produce the crops it had when he was little, before the bramble grew to choke it. I understood that he never wanted me to marry Jorda.

I understood that maybe, he'd wanted to give me the bell a long time ago, but had been too scared to do it. Why else would he have begged and called in so many favors from old friends to make sure I worked as a butcher?

I WALKED through Lesser Khaim dressed as an executioner.

Inside I was still me, Tana, weary and tired, struggling to see through the small slits in the leather hood over my face.

I'd called Duram down, and kissed him on his forehead before I had left.

"What was that for?" he'd asked, puzzled.

"Just know that I love you and your brother. I have to leave for an errand. But I will be back home soon."

After I sent him back upstairs, I'd opened the cedar chest in Anto's room and pulled out both his hood and heavy cape. They fit me well as I pulled them on, as Anto said they would. His canvas leggings slid off my waist, but a length of rope fixed that.

The axe lay in the bottom of the chest, the edged curve of the blade gleaming in the light.

It weighed less than it looked, and was well balanced in my hand. Heavier than the axe I used to chop wood with, but not anywhere as heavy as I had somehow imagined.

Now I rested the axe on my shoulder and walked down the banks of the Sulong.

I followed a fire crew down the stone steps. They wore masks and thick, double-canvas clothing. As they walked they pumped the primers on the back of their tanks, then lit the fires on the brass-tipped ends of their hoses.

When they flicked the levers, fresh flame licked out across the bramble threatening to creep over the stairs. Clumps of the thorny, thick creep withered under the assault.

Clearers followed close behind, chopping at the bramble, careful not to touch any of it lest they get pricked. Children scampered around with burlap sacks to pick up bramble seeds.

They stopped the burn when they saw me and stepped aside to let me down the path.

"If it's Alacan magic users you're sending to Borzai's judgment today," one of them called out from behind a mask as fearsome as mine, "then I salute you."

Others agreed in wordless grunts as they hacked at bramble with axes.

The ferry across the river dipped low to the water when I stepped aboard. The ferryman dug his pole deep into the muck and shoved us along the guide ropes that kept the raft from drifting downstream.

"Ain't the Alacan refugees causing the bramble creep," he muttered, and jutted his chin upriver.

I knew that. I could both see and smell the problem as the raft cleared a tall thicket of ossified bramble. When it wasn't cleared, the roots thickened, and hardened to become a singular and impenetrable mass.

And appearing behind that mass, far over the river Sulong, a half completed bridge soared from Khaim's side of the riverbanks. The unfinished structure hung in the air with no visible means of support, floating over the river as men worked on extending it toward Lesser Khaim day and night.

The stench of the magic holding the half-completed structure in the air wafted down over the river's surface: strong, tangy, and dangerous.

All that magic caused bramble to spring up all throughout Khaim and Lesser Khaim. People scraped it from their windowsills and fought it throughout their fields.

"Mark me," the man said with a final push to get us to the other side. "We'll end up like Alacan: choked with bramble and fleeing our city if we keep building that unholy thing."

I paid the ferryman his copper and stepped off onto the pier. He said those things only because he was bitter about losing his livelihood. There would be no place for him when people could simply walk the bridge.

I walked through Khaim, enjoying the taller marble and stone buildings and fluted columns. Lesser Khaim grew too quick: its buildings were cramped and close together, made of any materials that could be found. It was chaotic, and the Alacaner slums added the stench of cooking fires and sewage to what had once been lemon trees and pomegranates in bloom.

But my relaxation faded as I realized people scuttled away before me in nervousness. And it fled when I turned to the public square and the raised platform at the center where the executions were held.

Early crowds had already gathered. Vendors walked around selling flatbreads and fruits, and city guards waited by the steps.

They waved me on impatiently, and I saw the figure in chains between them. He turned, saw me, and his knees buckled. The guards held him up under his arms and laughed.

THE JOLLY Mayor himself came to the square and puffed his way up the stairs. His beady eyes regarded me for only the briefest of seconds, then fixed on the blade.

He smiled and moved closer. "Make this a good one, eh, Executioner?" He chuckled before I could even think to ask what he meant. Which was a good thing, as I wasn't sure I could reach for a deeper voice. I was far too nervous.

The guards dragged the prisoner up the stairs, sobbing and retching. They shackled him to the four iron rings on the floor of the platform, half bowed to the Mayor, and then retreated.

Chains tinkled as the prisoner moved, trying to look over his shoulder. "Please, please, have you no mercy? My sheep were dying of mouth rot, my family would have starved…"

The Mayor did not look at the man, but instead at the crowd. He cried out, for all to hear, "Khaim will *not* fall to the bramble, like the cities of the Empire of Jhandpara. Their failures guide us, and we call for the gods to forgive us for what we *must* do: which is to punish those who use forbidden magic, for they threaten every last one of us."

Then the Mayor turned to me and waved his hand.

A sound like a babbling brook came from the crowd. The murmur of a hundred or so voices at once. Behind that I heard the shifting of chains, and the sobbing of a doomed man.

I imagined either of my two sons laid out like this, begging for forgiveness. I imagined my Jorda's scrawny body there, his burn-marked fire crew arms pulled to either side by the chains.

I had to steady myself to banish these thoughts, so I wobbled a step forward.

I raised the axe high, so that I would only need to let it fall to do its work, and as I did, the crowd quieted in anticipation.

I LET the axe fall.

It swung toward the vulnerable nape of the man's neck as if the blade knew what it was doing.

And then the man shifted, ever so slightly.

I twisted the handle to compensate, just a twitch to guide the blade, and the curving edge of the axe buried itself in the man's back at an angle on the right. It sank into shoulder meat and fetched up against bone with a sickening crunch.

It had all gone wrong.

Blood flew back up the handle, across my hands, and splattered against my leather apron.

The man screamed. He thrashed in the chains, a tortured animal, almost jerking the axe out of my blood-slippery hands.

"Gods, gods, gods," I said, terrified and sick. I yanked the axe free. Blood gushed down the man's back and he screamed even louder.

The crowd stared. Anonymous oval faces, hardly blinking.

I raised the axe quickly, and brought it right back down on him. It bit deep into his upper left arm, and I had to push against his body with my foot to lever it free. He screamed like a dying animal, and I was crying as I raised the axe yet again.

"Borzai will surely consider this before he sends you to your hall," I said, my voice scratchy and loud inside the hood. I took a deep breath and counted to three.

I would not miss again. I would not torture this dying man any more.

I must imagine I am only chopping wood, I thought.

I let the axe fall once again. I let it guide itself, looking at where it needed to be at the end of the stroke.

The blade struck the man's neck, cleaved right through it, and buried itself in the wooden platform below.

The screaming stopped.

My breath tasted of sick. I was panting, and terrified as the Mayor approached me. He leaned close, and I braced for some form of punishment for doing such a horrible thing.

"Well done!" the Mayor said. "Well done indeed. What a show, what a piece of butchery! The point has well been made!"

He shoved several hard-edged coins into my hand, and then walked over to the edge of the platform. The crowd cheered, and I yanked my axe free and escaped.

But everywhere I turned the crowd shoved coppers into the pockets of my cape, and the guards smacked me on the back and smiled.

When I turned the corner from the square I leaned over a gutter, pulled the hood up as far as I dared, and threw up until my stomach hurt.

Afterwards, I looked down and opened the clenched fist without the axe in it. Four pieces of silver gleamed back at me from the blood-soaked hand.

I wanted to toss them into the stinking gutter. But then, where would that leave my family?

Guards ran past me, shouting orders. I didn't pay attention to whatever it was that had stirred them. But whatever they had shouted was repeated through the crowd, which began to fade away, their interest in executions lost in favor of something else.

I folded my fingers back over my payment, even though they shook, and began to walk back toward Lesser Khaim.

THE FERRYMAN looked nervous and intent on his work as he poled me across the river. He had unloaded a full raft, and people had shoved past me with determination.

He blanched when I offered him a bloody copper. "You keep it," he murmured. Then he looked at me again. "Are you sure you want to cross over right now, Executioner?"

I broke free of my daze. "What do you mean?"

The ferryman pointed a callused finger at the air over Lesser Khaim. "Raiders have attacked. Haven't you heard?"

A tendril of smoke snaked up over the jagged roofs and clustered wooden buildings.

"No. Whoever told you that must be mistaken," I told him. I'd lived my entire life on the edge of Lesser Khaim. The raiders would never strike this far north. There was nothing here for them, on the edge of the bramblelands that were once Jhandpara's great empire.

"Believe what you will," he said, as the raft struck the other side. A crowd rushed to the raft as I left it. I walked up the bank to Lesser Khaim, stepping around black tendrils of bramble scattered on the carved steps.

A screaming man smacked into me at the top. His left arm dangled uselessly, crushed. We both fell to the ground, and he scrabbled up.

"Damn you," I grunted, "what are you doing…"

"Raiders!" He shouted at me. "Raiders."

I sat up, pulling the axe close to me, and looked down the street. More smoke seeped into the tight alleyways between buildings.

And I could hear screams in the distance.

The streets were filling with people moving quickly for the river, their eyes darting about, expecting attackers in every shadow and around every alley.

"They're here to burn us to the ground," the man said. He was originally from Turis, I could hear it in his accent. His eyes seemed to be looking far away, as if he were reliving the horrors of the raider attacks that forced him to walk barefoot all the way to Lesser Khaim.

People jostled past us, a moving river of humanity headed for the riverbanks. "Where are they going?" I asked. They would drown in the river if the raiders got this far.

"Away," the man said, and ran off with them.

I pushed through the oncoming crowds. They split apart for an executioner, and if they did not, I used the bronze-weighted butt of the axe to shove them aside.

Five streets from the river, I had to turn away from my usual route home. Smoke choked the street, black and thick, and it spat people out who coughed and collapsed to the dirt, gasping for air.

"They set fire to the slums! Don't go down there," a woman with a flour-covered apron shouted at me.

I ignored her and ran through alleyways. I pushed through the doors of empty houses and climbed through windows to make my way around the burning sections of town, slowly getting closer to home.

I ran past the burning wrecks of the small farms of the Lesser Estates, my boots raising dust with each step. I could see the gnarled trees behind my house writhing in flame, and as I scrambled painfully over the stone wall, I saw the timbers give way and the roof fall in on itself.

The heat forced me back when I tried to run inside. I paced around the house like a confused animal. Stone cracked from the heat, and a screaming wail came from within. I ripped my hood off and shoved it into one of my pockets so I could breathe.

"Duram?" I cried. "Set?"

A blazing figure erupted from the front door, leaping onto the dusty ground and rolling around until the flames were extinguished.

It was Anto. His blackened form lay by my feet, rasping in pain. "Tana?"

I dropped to my knees. "Father?"

"It hurts," Anto whimpered. "It hurts. Please…" He looked up at me, eyes startlingly white against the blackened face.

The smell of burnt flesh filled my lungs. "You can't ask me…" I started to say.

"Please…" he groaned.

So I used the axe for the second time that day.

When it was done, I crawled on the ground and sobbed my despair, waiting for the house to finish burning. It was just. I had taken a man's life. Now mine was being taken from me.

I found Jorda's body while on my hands and knees. There was an arrow through his neck and a wineskin by his feet.

Drunkard he may have been. A disappointment to Anto, this was true. But the dirt was scuffed with footmarks. Small footmarks. He'd tried to protect my sons.

I kissed the three rings on my hand and prayed to Mara that my sons were alive, and as I did so, saw the scraped dirt of Set's dragged foot next to the hoofmarks leading off down the dirt road.

With an apology to Anto's lifeless body, a whisper of thanks to Mara, I got up and began to follow the tracks, axe gripped tight in both hands.

THE BURNT remains of Lesser Khaim's southern fringe faded away into the rocky hills of sparse grass and clumps of bramble as the day passed. Weariness spread through my knees, and the miles wore at me as I doggedly moved southward.

I plowed on. I knew that the hairy tentacles of bramble along the road brushing me would probably not pierce my canvas leggings. I had to move faster, not pick my way around bramble if I hoped to catch the raiders. I had to hope the leather apron would also help protect me from the bramble's malevolence.

At the crest of a hill scattered with boulders I looked back at the pyre that was now Lesser Khaim. Tiny figures formed a line by the river, passing along buckets of water to try and douse denser areas of town. The outer sections had become a black mass of skeletal building frames.

I turned from it all, walking down the other side of the hill, the axe weighing heavier and heavier.

At the bottom of the hill, turning onto the old cobble-stoned ruins of the Junpavati road, I caught up to the raiding party. The men rode massive, barrel-chested warhorses that looked like they could pull an oxen's plough. The raiders held their long spears in the air, like flagpoles, and their brass helmets glinted as they rode alongside a mass of humanity being herded south like sheep.

Somewhere in that sad, roped-together crowd, were my sons.

I wondered how many other townsmen had tried to fight the raiders? And how many lay dead on the dirt roads of Lesser Khaim with pitchforks or knives in hands.

I stared at the raiders. Only four of them had been left to march their captives along. No doubt the rest had ridden on ahead.

Four trained men.

And me.

I would die, I knew. But what choice did I have? They were ripping my family away. What person would run from their own blood?

I had killed already today, I thought, hefting the executioner's axe. I was dizzy from exhaustion, and the mild poison of the few bramble needles that had poked through my leggings threatened to drop me into bramble sleep. But I made my decision, and moved toward the raiders.

As I did so, I pulled the executioner's hood back over my face to protect myself from the taller clumps of bramble drooping off of the rocks.

I USED the rocks and boulders of the dead landscape to get close to the raider trailing the column of prisoners. I was stunned by how large the man's warhorse was. When its hooves slammed into the ground, I could feel them from twenty feet behind.

The hems of my cloak brushed bramble as I ran at the man's back, and the horse whinnied as it sensed me. The raider spun in his saddle, spear swinging down in an arc as he looked for what had spooked the horse, and he spotted me.

He realized I was inside the spear's reach, and he leaped off his horse to avoid the first high swing of my axe at his thigh, putting the horse between us. I ran in front of the giant beast to get at him, but before I could even raise the axe again, he attacked.

His red cloak flared out behind him, and the spear lashed out. I was slow, but I dodged the point. In response the man

flicked it up and smacked the top of my head with the side of the shaft.

"And what do you think you're doing?" the raider demanded. He sounded unhurried and calm.

"You stole my family," I said as my knees buckled from the blow to the head. I fought to stand, and wobbled slightly. Hoofbeats thudded behind me.

The raider used the spear to hit me on the side of my head before I could even raise the axe to try and block the movement. His movements would have been too fast for me even if I hadn't been tired from chasing them, or my blood filled with bramble poison. The blow dropped me to the ground, blood running down over my eyes inside the hood, blinding me.

"What do we have here?" a second raider voice asked, as feet hit the ground. My hood was ripped clear of my head.

The two raiders bent over me, dark eyes shadowed by their bronze helmets, spears pinning my cloak, and me, to the ground.

I blinked the blood out of my eyes and waited for death.

"It's a woman," the raider I'd attacked said.

"That's quite plain," said the other. "Should we kill her or take her with us?"

"She's too old to go to the camps or to sell."

The other raider nodded. "So we kill her?"

"She doesn't need to be part of the Culling," the older-sounding raider said. He shook his head. "No, she's too old to have children. She's no threat. Cripple her so she can't follow us, then leave."

The older raider remounted his horse and left.

The remaining raider and I stared at each, and then he reversed his spear. "The Way of the Six says that we should…"

I spat at him. The effort dizzied me. "I don't care about your damned Way of the Six, slaver. Do what you came to do."

He shrugged and slammed the butt of his spear into my ankle, crushing it.

As I screamed, he smacked my head. I fell back away, down into a patch of bramble the pierced my clothing. With so many bramble needles stuck to my skin calling me down to sleep, it was enough to easily throw me away from the world.

Part Two

I WOKE UP WITH A grunt in the dark, something creaking and swaying beneath me. I'd been dreaming about a younger Set, his large brown eyes looking into mine as he struggled so hard to stumble about, learning to walk.

He'd fallen, and I'd rushed out, shouting at him to be careful, and then I had woken up.

I felt for my forehead, but there was no pain or bump as I expected.

My ankle felt fine. I felt fine, except for the extreme slowness that remained with me from the bramble sleep. I'd fallen into it once before, as a child. My parents had found me in the field and pulled all the bramble needles from my skin: people fretted over me for nearly a week as I lay trapped in a world of dreams and darkness.

I licked my dried lips and sat up.

The world kept creaking back and forth.

I heard wheels turning underneath me.

I was inside a covered wagon of some sort. Daylight peeked through cracks in wooden walls and top. And I could taste fish and salt hanging in the air.

A bird screeched outside, and I realized I must be near the coast.

My axe lay near me, as did my leather hood. Which meant I was somewhere safe.

In a daze I crawled toward a large flap, and as I reached it a hand flung it aside, blinding me with daylight.

"Well, hello there," someone said gently. "I was just coming to check on you."

My eyes watered, as if they hadn't seen sunlight in weeks.

Strong hands gripped my arm. "Careful, or you'll fall off."

I sat on the back of a large wagon. A small deck ran around the rim of the vehicle. A woman my age, traces of gray in her hair, held my arm. Her trader tattoos, including a striking purple figure of the elephant god Sisinak holding the triple scales of commerce, ran up and down her forearms. "I'm Anezka," she said. She squatted on the platform jutting off the back. "I was bringing you some soup. Everyone's going to be excited to hear you woke up."

I moved out onto the platform with Anezka, still amazed that my ankle wasn't hurting. Behind the wagon I was laid out in, another wagon followed.

That wagon behind us was pulled by four massive aurochs. They looked like cattle, but far more muscular, and their long horns swooped well out before them like the prows of ships. Four aurochs also followed the back of the wagon I was on, resting from the strain of pulling, their flanks rippling and hooves thumping the ground as they plodded along.

Behind the wagon following us, was another, and then another, and then another yet again. I counted ten before the long train of wagons curved around a bend in a fine mist of kicked up dust. Each wagon featured its own unique, mottled purples and greens painted in patterns on their wooden sides. Many had carvings: depictions of markets and roads and maps of the world, all expertly chipped into their sides.

"This is a caravan," I said out loud, realizing it at the same moment I spoke it.

"This is *the* caravan," Anezka said. "You're traveling the spice road on the perpetual caravan. We move along the coast starting in Paika and go all the way to Mimastiva and even a little beyond, until the bramble of the east stops us with its wall. Then we turn back around again. There used to be many, all throughout the old Empire. Now: only us."

Mimastiva was on the coast, hundreds of miles south of Khaim. Paika lay on the coast as well, far to the west. I knew of a few who'd visited Mimastiva. Paika was said to have fallen to the raiders when I was still a child. These were cities that to me, were almost past the edge of the world.

"You said that people would be excited I was awake," I said.

Anezka's eyes widened. "Because you're the lady executioner, who met four Paikans in mortal combat. Everyone's been talking about you up and down the line."

"Paikans?" I asked.

"You northerners call them raiders."

"I didn't fight four raiders," I said with a frown. "I only took on one, and he beat me badly. But yes, there were four of them."

I looked down at my ankle. "How long have I been asleep?"

"You should see the Roadmaster," Anezka said.

"Why is that?" I asked.

"Because this is his wagon, and you are his guest," Anezka said, somewhat formally, but quite firmly.

With her arm to steady me, I grabbed the ropes along the outside of the covered wagon's rim, and walked toward the front.

As we approached the raised platform from where the aurochs were controlled, I could see up the line of the caravan. We were near the front. Muscled men with brass arquebuses stood on a fifteen paces long war wagon in front of us, with hammered metal shieldwalls protecting them.

Further ahead, a wagon with a large fire crew burned bramble away from the road edges, the roar of the flame carrying back over the air to us. The stench of the burned limbs wafted past.

I was a long way from Lesser Khaim.

THE ROADMASTER was a successful, rich, mountain of a man, robes draped across the heft of his belly.

But if I thought him jolly, that was a mistake. His smile was tight, controlled, and his eyes shrewd. This man saw more miles pass under the wheels of his home in a year than most ever traveled in a life.

And judging by the lines in his face, he'd had a long life doing this. Like Anezka, trader tattoos ran up and down his forearms, and his ears dangled with earrings.

He had no mustaches, his lips were shaved clean, like a refugee from Alacan.

I'd heard tales of the caravan, and the coastal spice route. Townsmen who travelled south to markets were told tales of the great market of Mimastiva by other townsmen who ventured that far south, and here I was, sitting on a wagon with the Roadmaster of the caravan himself.

"Welcome to the spice road," the Roadmaster said with a twitch in the corner of his lips. He did not hold the reins himself: that was a job for a young man in a loincloth with massive arms who sat next to him, the thick leather straps leading to the aurochs draped across his lap. He watched the road like an owl, his eyes never blinking.

"Thank you," I said, and brushed my skirts up to sit by him. Sitting higher than the bramble along the road meant that a soft sea breeze cooled my skin.

From this perch, I could see the road stretching out along the rocky coastline before us. The ocean, hundreds of feet below us, slammed and boomed against the wall of brown rock. And out beyond the spray, the green waves surged around pinnacles of rock shaped like the spires of castles. And beyond the spray and foam, the ocean stretched out forever: flat, unbreaking, the color of wintergreen leaves.

"It is a beautiful sight," the Roadmaster said, noticing my gaze.

"I never thought I'd see it in my life," I whispered. I wondered if Duram or Set had seen this, as they were being marched west.

I leaned forward and hid my face in my grief, and the Roadmaster leaned close and touched my shoulder. "What is your name, lady executioner?"

"Tana." I swallowed. "Tana the lost. Tana the homeless. Tana the abandoned. But not Tana the lady executioner. I'm not that thing."

"I am Jal," he said softly. "Where are you from Tana?"

"Khaim," I told him, and then I corrected myself. "Lesser Khaim."

"Ah, Khaim." He nodded. "I think I remember Khaim when I was just a boy. I was still sitting on my father's lap when he led the last caravan through. Sometimes I think I remember the start of that journey, or the greater cities of the Jhandparan Empire. I know I remember seeing a great palace that had fallen to earth, tilted, its foundational plane shattered like a plate! And the bramble, it gripped the city like a giant's fist, it did."

My grief broke a little, hearing his memories. "You are that old?"

Jal laughed at me. "I am that old. Yes. Hopefully old enough that I'll die before I lose the title of Roadmaster to the title of Bushmaster, which is what they will call me when even the spice road on this coast becomes choked by damned bramble."

I looked out on the road, and thought about what came next. "Where do you head?"

"Paika," the Roadmaster said. "And you will too."

He said this so firmly, I jerked to stare at him. "What do you mean?"

"The men who delivered you here said you attacked four Paikans on your own. They said you demanded your family back, and fought to the near death. So I have to imagine that a person who did that, would not then turn around and head back where she came from."

As he spoke, he turned and looked at me with a larger smile.

"I will not be going back to Lesser Khaim," I agreed.

"The men who brought you to me thought so. Paika is the greatest city in the west, and where your family most probably will be taken. And Paika is a carefully guarded city. You cannot enter without an examination, and papers, and a writ, unless you are like me and have dispensation. The Paikans fear people like you coming in to try and find their families. Yes, a person who attacks four of them would go to Paika with someone like me, who could get you inside, I think."

I shook my head in frustration. "I didn't attack all four of the raid… I mean Paikans. The stories are wrong."

"Of course they are. They're always wrong. Stories are for the listener, Tana. And it is what the listener makes of them that truly matters. The men who saw you attack the Paikans, they told us they found their courage. If one woman could attack four horsemen, then they could do the same. For two days and two nights they plotted, and then finally… attacked!"

I couldn't believe what I heard. But it had to be true, didn't it? Or I wouldn't be here. "And they succeeded?"

"They killed three of the Paikans and took their gold, their weapons, and their horses. Then one of them rode back to find you, where you were deep in the clutches of bramble sleep."

"How long," I asked. Jal waved a hand at me and ignored the question.

"When I saw them outside Mimastiva, they had you on a travois pulled behind a horse. They wanted to ride to Paika as fast as they could, so they gave me gold and a captive Paikan horseman. We will ransom him back to Paika for good coin."

Up ahead the aurochs plodded forward. The wagon groaned and creaked along.

"How long have I slept?" I asked again, fearing the worst.

"Three weeks, I think. Maybe a month. It could have been far, far worse. You are lucky to be alive."

I rubbed my arms. Would it be possible to find my family then, after a month? Or would they be scattered to even stranger lands? I bit my lip and looked at Jal. "The stories I have heard say the caravan is an expensive place to ride. Wherever I am, you can't carry any goods for trade, right? What are you asking for the price of my passage?"

I asked that, while fearing the worse.

"I'm not after your body," Jal muttered. "The coin and the prisoner your inspired friends gave me is enough. Or we would have left you asleep by the side of the road weeks ago. But you are right: no one in the caravan lies around. Well, unless they're in a bramble sleep. I will move you to another wagon, and you will work. Everyone in the caravan helps the caravan. That is our way."

I was relieved. "In Lesser Khaim I…"

Jal held up a hand to stop me. "Our needs are different than a town's. I don't care what you used to do. The caravan is a new life for you, until we reach Paika. Anezka says we need cooks in the lagging wagons to the rear. Or firewood scroungers. We need hagglers and movers with the trading teams, inventory managers to make sure nothing is being stolen…"

Now it was my time to interrupt. I thought about my fight with the raiders, and about the future I was reaching for. I was in a strange new land, and as Jal said, starting a new life.

I pointed at the wagon ahead of the fire crew. "Those men, with the arquebuses. Let me join them. I want to learn how to use those weapons. In Khaim there are just a handful of those old weapons, left over from the lords that once vacationed there, before the fall of Jhandpara. And here you have a team armed with them, it is very impressive."

Jal made a face. "Impressive? The magisters of Jhandpara would call down rocks from the skies and fly over their enemies to rain fire on them. *That* was impressive. These things are just loud tubes."

"I'm sorry," I said.

"No, no, I suppose you are right. The arquebus would be an interesting weapon for a lady…" and I could see the word 'executioner' lurk behind his lips, but then falter as I stared coolly at him. "Tana, to wield," he finished saying.

I looked at the road curving off into my future, filled with ruts and ropes of bramble. "Jal. The caravan goes all the way to Paika, then back to Mimastiva. You trade with them?"

"Of course. I am a man of trade," the Roadmaster said. "I work with anyone willing to pay a fair price for my goods, and leave me to the spice road. But my allegiance is to no one city. Most of us abandon such loyalties after years on the road, as cities rise and fall, come and go. Many of the families on the caravan have always been in the caravan, and will never rest until they reach the halls of Sisinak, if Borzai wills it and your life's trades have been judged honest. It is only there they will rest in the oasis markets, where the goods are never scarce, and the gold in your purse refills every night." Jal chuckled.

"So you are no friend of the… Paikans." I still had to hunt to use the right word. They had always just been known as 'raiders' to us in the north.

"I am no one's *friend*, I am a trader," Jal said. "If you doubt me, go see the Paikan chained away in our wagon. He will remain there until we get to Paika, and I negotiate a good price for his freedom."

"I may well do that," I said.

Jal raised his hands and clapped them together. "So. You want to use an arquebus. I will humor you. Bojdan! Come here."

One of the warriors looked back at us, set his arquebus down, then swung over the shields to drop to the road. He waited for the Roadmaster's wagon to approach, then climbed easily up onto the deck and walked up to us. "Yes?"

He was tall, with curled hair and a thick mustache. A massive scimitar hung on his left hip.

"This is Tana, the lady executioner. She will work with you to protect the caravan."

Bojdan looked me up, then down. "She is a woman," he said.

"Your powers of observation are astounding, Bojdan. It's a damned shame you aren't in charge of accounts, or haggling. Yes, she's a woman, it is plain for you and me to see. She is the woman who took on four Paikan soldiers by herself. Can you say the same?"

Again Bojdan regarded me. "Whatever you want, Roadmaster."

"You're correct, Bojdan. It *is* whatever I want. Take her back to a wagon with space to sleep, and teach her what she needs to know. And get out of my sight, by all the damned halls, get out of my sight."

Bojdan smiled. This was banter for them, the bluster that men exchanged. He turned around. "Let's go, Tana."

Jal cleared his throat. "Oh, and tell Anezka that Tana will not be joining them at the rear of the caravan to help out. She will be disappointed, I'm sure, but she is a capable manager, and will carry on."

I looked back at Jal. "Thank you."

"Good luck…" and he seemed to think about something, then smiled and said, "Executioness."

I shook my head and went back to fetch my things.

When Bojdan saw the axe, with the black stains in the handle, he nodded.

THE MUSCULAR warrior and I stood, our backs to scrub, rock, and bramble, and waited for the caravan to pass us by.

"Do you know anything about the raiders?" I asked.

"The Paikans? Dogs. All of them," Bojdan spat.

I liked the large man better for the reaction. "They took my family."

"They all but own the coast and more ever north. Ask Jal sometime, he'll piss himself complaining about the extortions they rip from him to 'allow' him to keep trafficking the spice road."

"They burned Lesser Khaim," I told him. "And my home."

"They have reached that far north? They call what they do the Culling. They believe it is their holy duty. You're lucky to live: they go after young women and children. Eliminate the breed cows, they say."

I stared at him. "How do you know all this?"

"Their preachers are all over Mimastiva, these days," Bojdan said. "Things will get worse in the East, now."

"Why do they do it?" I asked. What bizarre blasphemy did they preach?

"They blame us for the bramble," Bojdan said, and pointed at a small wagon with a single auroch pulling it. "The surviving Paikan of the four you faced is in that wagon…"

I cut him off. "I keep saying, I didn't face all four of them. It was just one, and he knocked me to the ground easily. They hobbled me and left me."

Bojdan nodded as we watched the wagon pass. For a moment, I thought about swinging aboard, and using my axe to kill the man inside. But Bojdan saw the thought crossing my face, and he smiled. "Don't think about sneaking off in the night to come and kill him. Jal will know it was you, and you wouldn't want to experience his anger if he were to lose his ransom."

It was better not to endanger my chance of getting to Paika, I thought. As the wagon passed on, I saw a glimpse of a figure sitting behind iron bars, his back to the world. I didn't recognize him as one of the two Paikans I'd fought.

"How long until we get to Paika?" I asked.

"Five weeks. Maybe six. The caravan is slow." Bojdan folded his arms. "We'll find you a place to sleep, and get your axe sharpened up. And then I guess I'm the one stuck training you so that the next time you decide to take on a group of Paikans, you might at least kill one of them."

FOR THE first two days Bojdan set me to walking alongside the caravan to get my feet back under me. We passed through more scrub and rock on the cliffs, but even in those two days, we began to move downhill, toward the ocean. We passed coves of sand, nestled in between the scallops of coast. My ankle was somewhat tender, and at night, I'd walk back to the wagon near the very end of the caravan and curse the pain.

But by the third day it was a dull ache, and Bojdan let me up into the guard wagon as we eased past a tiny fishing village perched over the ocean. Fishermen in rags raced up foothills, loudly hawking dried fish hanging from poles on their backs.

I noticed none of the other men on the guard wagon would look me in the eye. I could feel that they resented my being there.

We stood higher than all the caravan here, and I could see the five other guard wagons scattered throughout the snake-like convoy behind us.

"We used to have scouts running out ahead, beside, and lagging behind," Bojdan told me. "But Jal cannot afford it anymore. So we must be more vigilant than ever."

As he said that, he looked around at the villagers to our side, pressing close to the wagons, shouting and trying to barter as the caravan stolidly moved on.

I pointed at the gilded, brassworked arquebus Bojdan had over his shoulder. "But what about that? Isn't it a good weapon?"

"All weapons are good, if used properly," Bojdan said. He handed me the device. "It is loud, and almost anyone can use it, with some training. It sends bandits scurrying well enough."

It was heavy, and clumsy in my hands. I looked down the long barrel, its surface etched with thin, serpentine dragons. "I want to learn how to use this properly..."

He smiled.

I learned how to pour the powder, light the matchlock, and raise the arquebus to the side of the shieldwall to balance the ever-heavy barrel.

Powder was expensive, so Bojdan drilled me for the day without it. Over and over again I mimed putting in powder, putting in shot, tamping, then setting the gun on the ledge and aiming. I did it until my shoulders were sore.

"Look past the barrel," Bojdan urged, "to your target. That tree right over there. They are not accurate like a crossbow, or arrows, but you should still make the effort to aim."

This time the gun was loaded. The acrid burning match, pinched between the serpentine lock, had been pulled back and was ready to strike. All I had to do was pull the trigger, and the burning fuse would descend into the pan.

"Okay, fire it," Bojdan said.

I did, and the world exploded in light and smoke. "Sons of whores," I shouted, startled, and when the smoke cleared I saw a mess of shredded leaves and some broken branches far to the right of where I had aimed. And my shoulder hurt.

Bojdan's men laughed at me. "It's got a kick, yeah?"

But Bojdan didn't laugh. "Clean it, get a new one in, try again. Same tree!"

I reloaded rapidly, but not quick enough. The tree was almost obscured by the Roadmaster's wagon by the time I set the barrel on the shieldwall.

Bojdan grabbed it. "That was not bad, but not quick enough. So let's not shoot our employer with stray shot today. Shoot *that* tree."

I aimed at our sides again, and this time I was expecting the unholy roar of the weapon. Smoke burnt my face, and tears stung my eyes, but pieces of shot had fanned out and hit the tree I'd aimed at.

"Good," Bojdan said.

And then it was back to walking alongside the caravan for me.

IN THE second week, after more drills, Bojdan decided I could handle the arquebus well enough. We had left the coastal cliffs long behind us, and wound our way through soft plains near the ocean's edge. Trees, and further inland, woods, began to hem the road we traveled on, not just bramble and brush. "You know as much as us about the arquebus," he said. "Now it's time to think about close quarters. I will teach you to use your axe."

For this we left the caravan, once I'd retrieved the executioner's axe. We walked out into the woods as the wagons slowly rumbled past. Bojdan came with his scimitar, which was always at his side, and a small round shield he'd taken from the wagon's wall.

He looked me up and down. "You may think that because you are a woman that you are not a match for my men in the caravan. But if a one hundred pound warrior came to me, I would not turn him away merely because my men weigh twice what he does. I would, however, have to understand how best to use him. He is a tool. Some tools are large and heavy, useful for clubbing and smashing things. Some are thin daggers, useful for stabbing quickly."

This was the longest thing I'd heard him say, and it sounded carefully thought out, like a speech. "Did you think of how you would say this all last night, as you sat sentry?" I asked him.

"Shut up. There are hard lands we will pass through, and we will be attacked, and you will protect the caravan." He pulled his shirt apart to show scars on his chest, then pushed his sleeves up to show a wicked scar that cut deep into his upper arm, biting into the muscle there. "Whether you be a trained warrior, or an old lady, the skill of fighting lies not in what you can pick up, but in how much flesh you carve, and how well you will carve it, Tana. No one cares whether the person who does this is large, small, woman, or man. Even the best die suddenly on the battlefield. Death is death."

That was a true thing. But I held the axe out in my two hands. "You want me to use this axe, not a sword? Or a scimitar like you?"

Bojdan tapped the hilt of his blade. "Do you have a sword? Have you suddenly come into money, and can afford to buy one from someone here in the caravan?"

"No," I muttered.

"Then," he said, "it will be the axe, because it is what you have. I have held it, while you were sleeping. It is well balanced. It is light, and easy to wield. Hold it two handed, just like when chopping wood. And remember, you hold a unique weapon."

He moved my hand up a little, and then the other down. "A unique weapon?" I asked.

"Most men hold their shield with the left hand. With your axe, it is easy to switch it to a left handed strike, easier than learning to use a sword with your left. And you have a swing that comes easy to their unprotected side." He held his shield up to demonstrate. "Swing slowly."

Like chopping at a tree from the left, I did, and I could see what he meant. He had to move aside to get the shield in front of him. "I'm making you move around," I said.

"You're controlling the fight. From the first swing. There are other things you can do with the axe. For example, you can swing it past them and yank back, getting their neck with the downward facing edge of the axe's point. You can stab at them with the upward point of the blade. Spike them with the side away from the blade shaped so conveniently just like a spearpoint. Use the axe as a hook, to sweep them off their feet."

There was more. And halfway through the slowly shown moves, I stopped. "You know a great deal about fighting with axes."

Bojdan paused. "It's a peasant's weapon... and my first."

"Why do so few use it then?" I asked. "Everyone has one."

Bojdan thought about it, as if for the first time. "It's not the weapon of a warrior, but of the low peoples. It's for chopping trees and bramble, not flesh. That is what fighters say. Did the guards in Khaim work for their meals, or do nothing but soldier?"

"No," I shook my head. "They only soldiered."

He grinned, and warmed to subject. "So whether mercenaries or trained soldiers, it's the people who hold weapons who choose what they use the most. And they are not the same people who farm. So the axe isn't seen as a battle weapon."

I understood. "And that is good for me."

"Maybe," Bojdan shrugged. "There are many unusual weapons on the field. People who spend their lives loving weapons bring their preferred lover to the field of play. But it is not those small things that determine a battle. That is decided by things that take place long before foes meet."

I perked up. Bojdan commanded the fighting men of the caravan. It sounded like he had seen more combat than just scaring off bandits. "Like what?"

"It is how many soldiers are raised," he said. "Your axe will do you no good against a well aimed arrow. But an archer would have trouble escaping the jab of a sword. And so on. It is the mix of weapons and people, and how many you wield. It is how fresh they are. How healthy. Valor and intention are good for the heat of a battle, but if you are vastly outnumbered, there is only so much bravery can do."

I hefted the axe and thought about it. Bravery while charging the four Paikans had only gotten me beaten and left on the ground. "You need to win the battle before your first stroke."

Bojdan grinned. "Yes. And speaking of strokes, right there is a sapling we can take back for firewood for the cooks. Remember, chop from your left, the tree's right, to get past its shield."

"What shield?" I asked.

Bojdan walked past me even as I said that and strapped his shield to a branch that jutted out enough to be used as a temporary arm.

"Get to it!" he ordered.

And I took on the small tree as if it were a raider, or as I now thought of them, a Paikan, swinging past the shield and biting the axe into the meat of the sapling's bark over and over again, until it toppled forward and Bojdan yanked me out of the way.

"Never get so focused that you forget what else is around you," he said, as the tree struck the ground beside us.

FOR FOUR weeks we continued. Slow moving practices against each other, and fast ones when I faced more trees.

Bojdan carved a blunt axe out of wood for me, swaddled with cloth, and a light wooden scimitar padded just the same for himself.

With these we dueled in the ever thickening woods beside the caravan. The road began to slowly move back away from the coast, into the foothills. The ever-present smell of salt faded away, and we stopped passing seaside villages.

Few towns existed here in the thick overgrowth, due to bramble. Only a few solitary homesteads fought back, alone, becoming trapped by the increasing thicket and bramble just miles north of the road.

Occasionally we saw dim figures watching us go past, and the guards fingered their arquebuses, but nothing ever happened.

For a big man Bojdan moved damnably fast, constantly bruising my ribs and shoulders as we practiced, even slamming the padded scimitar down on my neck with swipes of his practice weapon.

Every time he hit me he'd mutter 'dead,' in a toneless voice.

But by the fourth week, he stopped saying that and moved on to 'maimed.'

After we fought, we'd run to catch back up to the caravan, sitting on the most rearward defense wagon, panting and catching our breath.

I SLEPT in a bunking wagon, filled with slat beds mounted on the walls. Ten women shared the tiny space, but I hardly knew them, even after four weeks. Except for Anezka, who'd been there as I woke up from my bramble sleep.

I came to the wagon always tired after Bojdan's training. I would crawl right into my bunk and fall sleep.

Bojdan and his men never saw me weaken. I'd worked among men in the butcher shops enough to know their minds. To know that to show weakness, tears, or anything other than humor and rage was to invite judgment.

But alone in the bunks, when sleep failed me, and I was alone with nothing more than the sounds of snoring women and the darkness that pressed against me, then I would sometimes surrender to tears as I thought about Set and Duram.

Because of that, I feared being alone with my mind. So I trained every moment I could, worked every second I could bear.

At first the women in the bunking wagon did not speak to me, or even meet my eyes, until the oldest, a lady with a leathery weathered face called Alka, asked if maybe I was fighting with Bojdan because I was not really a woman.

"I bore two children the Paikans took," I told her. "Torn from me like the old healer tore them from my body when they both refused to come easily. Would you have me expose myself to everyone in here to prove you wrong?"

I grabbed the hems of my skirts as if to raise them.

Alka shook her head quickly, scandalized, and the younger girls in the wagon laughed at her. "Of course she's a woman," the one called Anezka said. "She is the Executioness, remember? Not the Executioner!"

I shook my head at Jal's name for me. "Don't call me that," I asked. "I am just Tana."

The women settled at Anezka's berating. Anezka was, I had found out, a Quartermaster. The large mass of caravaners in the trailing edge provided the needs of the whole human train. Anezka and others like her handled accounting for supplies, and kept the trade goods under lock and key.

"There's the Roadmaster," she had explained once over a stewpot hanging from the balcony of the bunking wagon as we ate, "and then there's the Quartermasters. We really run it all."

The more I listened to the women chat in the wagon, the more I realized they were the grease that kept the caravan's wheels from seizing.

There were questions and pieces of information constantly bandied around me between the bunks: whose aurochs needed better feed? How fast was the caravan going? By the way, Anezka had noted a couple days ago, the flour was getting low, if they didn't get some barrels refilled, they'd run out in a week.

All these things and more these women knew.

Jal directed the caravan, but my bunkmates made the caravan a living creature.

And I was not one of them, though with the exception of Alka, they all treated me with careful politeness.

At the start of the fifth week, Bojdan sent me out with Anezka and three other women for water, as one of the casks had sprung a leak.

"We are near a small river that runs beside the road," he said. "Keep a guard. It's a safe area, but be careful."

Up and down the caravan flags whipped up onto small wooden masts at the rear of the wagons, giving the order to slow their pace.

Anezka and her three companions pulled along a two wheeled cart with them, which had three empty barrels on it. They laughed and joked as we moved down a narrow dirt path through the trees out of sight of the caravan, to the babble of the tiny stream.

"I like to oversee where the water comes from," Anezka said. "Sometimes these three get timid and don't want to wade clear out to the center where it's freshest."

"It was just once," one of them protested.

"We all suffered for it for a week," Anezka said. She looked over at me. "Will you leave us, when we get to Paika?"

"Yes." I walked beside her, and I looked around the forest as she talked.

"That's a shame. You could spend forever in that strange city, and never find someone," she said.

"You've seen it?" I asked.

"Right after I joined the caravan to see the world, and Jal was negotiating the rights to travel in their territory," Anezka said. "Building on building crammed into mazes of leaning streets. It's on a hill, and everything looks ready to fall over on top over everything else. And it goes on and on, from the foothills and up."

We reached the river, and I helped her pull a barrel from the wagon and roll it into the river with a splash. Anezka guided it to the center, her skirts knee-deep in the strong current. "Well, if they are there to be found, I will find them. And if they are not to be found..."

"Then what?" Anezka asked.

"I will kill the bastards that killed them," I said quietly.

"That is good," said one of the other women. "You do what few of us can. Most of us lost families to the Paikans, or our husbands. That's why we joined the caravan. What else were we to do?"

Anezka nodded. "They cull us. Or they take our youngest to large camps on some of the islands in their harbors, and off the coasts where we can never get to them. It's there that they teach them the Paikan ways and thoughts."

Everyone nodded. "Paikan ways: they're growing and growing."

Anezka then stopped the barrel back up. I moved to help her roll it, but she pointed.

Five men had slipped out of the shadows of the trees on the opposite bank, hardly twenty feet from us, and I hadn't noticed them. They had old, rusty swords, and were dressed in little more than rags.

Realizing they had been seen, they splashed awkwardly across the hip-deep water at us, swords in hand.

I picked up my axe. "Run for the caravan, but if they catch you, resist them any way you can," I shouted. I saw the grins on the men's faces as their splashing steps soaked their torn clothes. "Go!"

So much for vengeance, I thought, my heart pounding. I would die slowing these attackers down enough so that Anezka and her friends could get to safety.

Well, there were worse things to spend a life on.

I only hoped my sons would forgive me.

The men did not realize I'd picked up an axe, and I let my body shield it from their view.

Until they got close. Then I drew it from behind me and swung at the nearest man. He had his sword up already, as his compatriots ran past, leaving him to deal with just me.

After blocking his swing, I slid the axe down the blade, then shoved it forward, puncturing his stomach with the spike at the top of the axe's curve.

We both looked surprised that it had worked, and then I shoved him free to lie in the river, crying and groaning as his stomach spilled into the formerly clean river water.

The four men had caught themselves four struggling women and were laughing.

I ran, almost tripping over my skirts, and raised my axe up into the air and buried it into the lower spine of the first man I caught up to. Anezka, pinned underneath, screamed loudly enough the three remaining men paused. They looked over as the man on top of her rolled off. He began to spasm and gush blood now that the axe had been yanked free.

The three others shoved the women away, and began to move at me.

Bojdan hadn't taught me how to take on three opponents at once.

But he had taught me that a fight was won before the fight began. Digging deep inside I calmed myself and met their gazes with a grin.

It was an anticipatory grin. As if the first two men I had just killed were no more than an appetizer, and this was about to be a course I was looking forward to.

Never mind that I had killed one half because he expected no real resistance, and the other because his back was turned.

"Who are you, lady?" one bandit asked.

And Anezka stepped behind me. "Can't you tell by the damned blade!" she cried out indignantly. "This is the Executioness!"

They looked at the axe, and I wiped the blood from its edge with my thumb and tested the sharpness.

When I looked back up at them, I saw I had won this battle, for there was fear there now. "The one who faced an entire party of Paikans," one of them asked.

"Yes, that one," Anezka said.

I walked forward, axe in hand, and the nearest man threw his sword at my feet. "I surrender my weapon," he said.

After a moment, the others did too.

"Pick up the swords," I ordered Anezka. She did, and handed them to the other women. "Run for the caravan," I whispered to her. "Get Bojdan and some of his men, quick!"

"Yes," Anezka replied, wide-eyed. And she spun and ran.

I turned back. Were there more men out in the woods? If I let these three go, would they come back for their revenge? "You three, see those barrels?" I asked.

They nodded.

"Get them aboard that cart, and pull it over here," I ordered. They did so, quickly and with some grunting, and once the cart was in front of me, I hopped on. "Now follow those women back to the road. Do not give me any excuses to take your heads."

They again nodded.

Sitting on top of a barrel, I watched them closely as they pulled the cart through the forest to the road. I remained calm outwardly, but inside my heart raced, my breath came short, and I was terrified of every shadow in the trees.

When we broke out onto the road, the caravan was still slowly passing us by.

Bojdan and three of his men rushed up to us. They looked at my prisoners with some shock.

I leapt down from the cart, my bloodied axe over my shoulder, and grabbed Bojdan by the arm. "I would talk to you over here," I said, and lead him around to the other side of a wagon, dodging the aurochs.

Then I let my legs fold, and my breath come in staggered gasps. "Piss on them," I spat, my voice breaking with fear. "There were five of them and one of me. Five!"

Bojdan held me up. "Come, you need to go lie down," he said gently. "You've done enough."

He walked me back down the road to a bunk wagon, empty of occupants. "What are you..." I asked.

But he shoved me up onto the platform. "Go inside, rest for a moment, gather your thoughts. I will deal with these remaining men."

My hands shook, and I watched him pace along the wagon for a moment, then dart through the caravan and disappear.

I crept into the darkness and curled up on someone's unfamiliar smelling bunk. I kept curling up until my body could bear being squeezed by itself no more.

When Bojdan finally came back, it might have been after an hour, or five. All I'd done was stare at a chipped piece of wood on the wall. I'd felt that the wagon had stopped. Maybe the whole caravan had. I knew dimly something was going on, but until that moment, hadn't cared about finding out.

Bojdan said nothing, but sat in the back of the wagon and waited until I rolled over to look at him.

"It was different," I finally said. "Not like the execution, or when I went for the raider in anger."

Bojdan just sat there.

I continued. "I had to stay in control, and calm. I had to win the fight first."

"You did well," said Bojdan. "Never doubt it. You are a good fighter."

"Why did the caravan stop?" I asked. "It's not supposed to stop, right?"

Bojdan grimaced. "Our way is blocked by a scouting party. Somewhere out in the woods, north of us, a man called Jiva has been raising the discontented to fight against the Paikans. You met five of their number earlier. They're all from culled villages and towns out there."

"What do they want?"

"Food, weapons, anything we have that we can trade. Their stores ran low in the march south through bramble and forest. They look hungry enough to attack us for our stores. And Jal is reluctant to trade with them, as the Paikans will be upset. So... negotiation continues."

"Ah." I turned back over.

After many long moments I twisted around and found Bojdan still there.

"I will be fine," I said.

But the warrior shook his head. "Few are ever truly 'fine' after what you just did, after what we do. We can get back to being a reflection of our former self, but it's somehow not quite the same. And only another like us understands what we mean."

"I know, but I want to be left to myself for now," I told him. "Just for now."

"I will send for you when it is time for the night watch," he said. "I will need all the warriors I can fetch by my side. Particularly if Jal and the scouts can't come to an agreement."

I felt the wagon shake as he stepped out onto the road.

Part Three

ANEZKA CRAWLED INTO THE wagon as the sun left its place in the sky and woke me up. "Bojdan needs you."

"Thanks." I crawled out of bed, and before I could leave the wagon, Anezka grabbed my shoulders.

"Thank *you* for saving us," she said.

I wasn't sure what to say, but I hugged her back. "You should carry a dagger, and practice how to stab someone," I whispered to her. "All of you should."

"We're just talliers and cooks and supply keepers, we're not... you, Executioness."

I sighed. "I'm just like you. I'm in the middle of my life. A mother who helped in a butcher shop. There is nothing special about me, I swear to you."

But I could see Anezka didn't believe me.

I crawled out of the wagon and got to the road where lantern light showed a small group of muddy men in tattered peasant's clothes, carrying crates of vegetables and dried meats, trudging quickly down the road. They intermixed with the caravan as they did so.

They all carried simple swords. I saw a single crossbow-man in blue cloth further down, surcoat slapping the backs of his knees.

Their faces did look gaunt as they slipped off into the shadows just past the caravan's edges.

At the front of the stalled caravan, Bojdan stood with Jal by the Roadmaster's wagon. They welcomed me into their discussion.

"One of those scouts says there are Paikans coming down the road," Bojdan told Jal. "They are a half hour away. We need to get moving again so that everything looks normal."

"Don't fret, Bojdan. The Paikans have always respected the neutrality of the caravan. I'm more worried about Jiva's men here. If a few hungry idiots rush our wagons for stores, or loot, and we fight back, this will be an expensive mess," Jal snapped. He eyed the passing remnants of the scouts. "Is that the last of them?"

"Yes," Bojdan said.

"Good. Send the command, we're moving along. Relax Bojdan. Relax."

"I'll relax when the Paikan party moves past us to their destination," Bojdan said. "If they know about Jiva, we don't want to get caught in the middle."

"Yes, yes," Jal said quickly. "I know. So let's get those command flags snapping, guardsman."

Bojdan ran forward, shouting orders. The fire wagon to the front lurched forward, and then Bojdan's wagon of guards followed. A green flag with a triangle in the middle lurched up the pole with a swaying lantern at the top. All along the column the same flag raised, and the caravan began to move.

I went to follow Bojdan, but Jal grabbed my shoulder.

"We have a Paikan prisoner in a wagon and everyone in the caravan knows about it. I want you to guard him. Now that there are armed Paikans coming down the road, there are those in the caravan that might release him who are friendly to the Paikan cause. I don't want to ransom him until we get to the city, we get more for him that way."

I lowered my voice. "I couldn't raise my hand against someone from the caravan."

Jal laughed. "Oh, you won't have to, Tana. If I let it be known the Executioness is guarding our prisoner then I doubt anyone in the caravan will be interested."

"I don't like that name," I protested, but Jal held up a hand.

"That is too bad, it has stuck. Now take your axe and go," Jal ordered. "What in all the damned halls are we doing moving so slowly! You said it was *urgent* we get out of here, Bojdan, not something to do in our damned spare time."

"You have come around to my way, I see," Bojdan shouted back.

Jal grumbled and climbed up on the Roadmaster's wagon while I stalked back down the length of the caravan for guard duty.

AFTER I'D climbed into the wagon and sat on the bench against the wall, the Paikan stirred. He crawled to the bars that kept him prisoner and looked out into what he could see of the night from his prison.

"I saw those scouts," he said evenly. The dull red flicker of lanterns swaying in the wagon's ceiling pulled the Paikan's figure out of the dark.

I said nothing.

The man sat, his side against the bars. "Have it your way. They are angry at us, for what we did. And yet they still haven't learned the lesson we strive to teach the world. They think they can take us in battle, but all they will do is throw away their lives."

I didn't want to talk to the man. I felt like he would force that old me, the unskilled me, the unblooded me, to reemerge from where she'd been pushed over the last weeks. The me that would be scared of him.

But I felt calm sitting here in the dark, the axe across my lap. I was a deep river, unhurried and powerful, not a frothy shallow stream. "And what lessons do you think you teach the world," I asked. "Other than your barbarism."

He jumped back. "You're a woman."

I smiled. I had control of this conversation, not him. There was no fear in my voice when I said, "Yes, so I've always been told."

He moved closer to the bars, and looked down at the axe on my lap.

"Are you *that* woman? The one I hear them call the Executioness? From the far East?"

"My name is Tana, of Lesser Khaim," I told him. I saw his shadow relax. "I was once a butcher, and married to a husband called Jorda. My sons were Duram, and Set. And yes, some call me the Executioness."

I could hear him draw in his breath as I claimed the name for the first time. "Are you here to kill me?"

I imagined him here in this cell, hearing that someone whose life he'd destroyed and children he'd stolen, was amongst the caravan. He must have had many sleepless nights.

Which was good.

"I am here to guard you, for now." I placed the butt of the axe against the floor, and folded my hands around the top. "Killing you now would not help me understand where my family may be."

He remained quiet for a while, so I took the axe and hit the bars with it. He jumped back. "Your family is lost to you," he snapped.

"Why do you say that?" I demanded, getting off the bench I'd sat on. "I didn't come this far to turn back!"

He moved away from the bars.

I moved closer. "I will not kill you, but I think maybe I will come to maim you before we reach Paika. I think an arm would be acceptable to me. You could still talk after that, right? I don't know, because I've never tried anything like that before. But I think an arm is a fair thing, after all, what is an arm compared to a family? We can live both our lives incomplete."

The Paikan raider stepped forward to the bars. "You'd risk it all, for this quest?"

I looked him in the eyes. "Yes."

"I have nothing good to tell you," he said. "Because I doubt you'll catch your children."

"You would have sold them by now?" I asked. "Is that what you do, you twisted creatures…"

"No one young is sold," the Paikan said, a note of outrage seeping into his voice. "Their minds are moldable, they can be taught. The young can be saved."

"What are you talking about?" I demanded.

"Your sons will have been taken to the aftans of Paika. There they are taught the Way with hundreds, no thousands, of youths from all over these diseased lands, every day, until the moment their minds crack open, and the inherent truth of the Way falls upon them. It is then that they earn the right to go to the Southern Isles, far from these coasts."

"Why would they want to go there?"

"A pilgrimage. To see the lands where the Way is all. To see where we came from, long before we took the city of Paika and made it our home. Your children will be closer to the end of their time at the aftan than at the beginning, now."

I wanted to hit him with the butt of the axe, but restrained myself. He was talking. Even if I didn't want to hear it, he was talking about what was happening right now to Duram and Set.

"Why?" I asked. "Why do your people do all this? Why steal my children?"

The prisoner's voice crackled with anger. "Because you don't deserve them." He grabbed the bars. "We have them heavily guarded and protected. And when the Way gives itself over to them, they will leave for their pilgrimage. And when they return, they will bring light to this darkened land you have created."

"What are you talking about?" I sat face to face with his fiery anger.

"Look around you," he whispered. "Your towns are fallen, bramble eats and chokes at all you do. And still you can't release yourselves from the grip of the sickness that causes it."

"Magic?" I asked. "You're talking about magic. It's outlawed. That is why I was an executioner. We control it."

"You control nothing, or your greatest empire would not have fallen. You are all sick with magic's use."

"And you are not?" I said.

"No," he insisted. "Your peoples try to use fear and death to stop magic but it will always continue. The individual will always have a use that seems to be needed, even when compared to the good of all. You have no true beliefs like the Way to guide you. Just heapings of gods that take you long after you destroy everything in *this* life. As long as your afterlives are pleasant, what reason do you have to ever stop the bramble?"

"You are all missionaries, here to spread this thing you call the 'Way' by kidnapping our children? Is that what this madness is all about? Is that why you have destroyed my family and my town?" I wanted to kill him then.

"It is to save you from yourselves," he said sadly, as if I were a child who did not know any better. "You want to know why I came here, to this cursed land? Let me tell you. One morning, far off in the Southern Isles, I woke up and found a small, gray thorn growing in the wall around my yard. And over time it grew, its needles spreading. And chopping it back did nothing, its roots continued to spread. One day my wife, and my son took it upon themselves to pull up every root by hand, and slipped into the deepest sleep, and then from there to death. That is why I am here, Executioness."

He trembled, and I understood his rage. "I'm sorry to hear about your family."

The Paikan continued. "I'm here because my people forgot magic, and left it behind us when we settled the islands and left the Northern Coasts. I'm here because we believe Borzai judges all that we do, including what we do to this world that the gods love. I'm here because like the Jhandparan Empire, you can't help yourselves, and we suffer all together as a result. So we try to stop you from killing us, as well as yourselves."

"This is all about magic. And bramble," I said.

"What else could it be about?" the man inside the cell asked.

A trumpeting sound came from the distance.

The Paikan sucked in his breath. "The cavalry is here," he said. "That is no small Culling party, but an army. You should leave this place, and go back to where you came from. Start a new life."

"I am too old to start a new life, or family," I said.

"Then that is a shame," he said. "But there is nothing for you in Paika."

"My children are in Paika," I hissed. "There is *everything* for me there."

I could hear a distant thudding. "They're not stopping, they're not stopping," someone screamed from up the caravan.

I stepped away from the inside of the wagon and pulled myself up the side so I could look down the road.

Forms lumbered out of the dark in front of the fire crew's wagon. Elephants with armored tusks swinging from side to side as they charged forward.

They ran. And they were, indeed, not stopping.

The aurochs harnessed to the wagons up front screamed and threw themselves against their harnesses. The Roadmaster's wagon toppled over as the beasts fought to get free.

Bojdan's men raised their arquebuses as one, and fired. The leading elephant shrieked and reared, then brought its massive feet down on the wagon, splintering and destroying it, throwing men from it like so much chaff in the wind.

I jumped down and ran alongside the caravan toward them, seeing more elephants moving through the large cloud of smoke left by the fired arquebuses. The dominating creatures had slowed down in the smoke. They walked three abreast, and four rows deep.

I saw Jal and Bojdan duck for cover behind the Roadmaster's wagon as a sudden flurry of crossbow bolts thwacked into the wooden sides and clattered off the road.

I joined them, slamming my shoulder next to Jal's against the ruins of his wagon. "I don't understand," he repeated. "I don't understand. They couldn't have found out we sold those rebel scouts supplies so soon, could they, Bojdan?"

The warrior shrugged. "There are many other sins they could have decided to call you on, Jal."

"But I bribed them all, Bojdan!" the Roadmaster spat. "We make them rich. I use none of the magics they despise."

"Can you guarantee that no one else in this caravan ever used any magic?" Bojdan asked.

An elephant bellowed. Jal glanced over his shoulder and muttered, "Borzai be merciful when I meet you today."

Bojdan looked behind us. "We need to retreat," he said. "They're getting ready for another charge."

The remains of the guard wagon exploded and lit the entire night. The fireball blistered us with heat and roiled overhead, blunted by the now burning carcass of the Roadmaster's wagon "Arquebus powder," Bojdan explained, with a sudden smile. "That will give us cover, now run!"

Elephants shrieked, and I could hear cursing.

Several arrows clattered around as we stood and ran. Jal gurgled, then pitched back, looking like a pincushion: his ample body pierced from all angles by crossbow bolts. He was still alive, amazingly, crawling along the road and swearing.

Paikan crossbowmen charged us from the side of the road where they'd walked around the burning debris. Bojdan ran at them as they reloaded their devices. He began slicing arms, throats, and bellies. I buried my axe into the chest of a startled man who pointed his sword at me.

But before we could do more, the ground shook, and out from the smoke of that last great explosion, the war elephants charged once more. Crossbowmen fired down at us from wooden platforms on the elephants' backs.

A Paikan in purple robes stalked over to the Roadmaster, a crossbow in hand. "You have sinned against all," he shouted. "You have failed to keep control of your people, and failed to keep them from using that which harms us all."

"Get away from the caravan," Bojdan said, shoving me away from what was about to happen. "It's all…" he didn't finish his sentence: a bolt buried itself in his neck.

He fell. I lunged forward, to go to him, but bolts struck the ground around me.

The battle is won long before the fighting, I thought. And this was a lost battle.

I spun and ran for the forest to the north of the road, where it looked thick and I thought I could lose myself.

THE TRUMPETING of the war elephants faded as I pushed deeper into the wild. There was some bramble here, I could feel the soft needles tugging my skirts as I brushed past. But I couldn't slow down, despite the dark. I could hear the sounds of someone following me, the glow of their torch bobbing through the dark shadows far behind.

With no light, I could only walk so fast without smacking into trees and branches.

There were three torches now, I saw with a glance back. They gained on me, as they could see what was in front of them.

Every step north away from the road, every minute bumping through the scrub, took me further from Paika, and my sons.

I began to regret the time spent enjoying the slow wend of the caravan along the road. The sweet smell of the ocean. The comfort of food, and of Bojdan's company.

Yes, I missed him. It was a piece ripped away from me. Not like the piece missing inside me that was my family. But it was another cut that left me hardening up, like bramble when it wasn't totally killed.

As I ran, I hardened even further than I had before. I pushed through tall grass and broke out into a clear area on the edge of a small lake. Pebbles crunched under my feet.

How long had I kept moving through the woods? An hour?

If I kept running, the Paikans with torches would exhaust me, then easily capture me.

So I crouched low by the grass's boundary, axe readied, to make my stand.

The first man broke from the grass, his torch held high in one hand, spear in another. His spiked helmet glinted in the torchlight, as did the rest of the armor buckled to him.

I slammed the axe point first, as if it were a spear, into the face of the helmet as it turned, suddenly suspicious, in my direction.

Blood splattered the shaft of the axe, and the torch and spear clattered to the pebbles. I stepped back as the other two Paikans slowly parted the grasses on either side of me.

They looked down at their dead comrade, and kept their distance, but moved along the grass boundary to cut me off from running away. They tossed their torches down to the pebbles and gripped their spears in both hands. "You're a woman," the one to my left said, surprise in his voice. "Why do you face us?"

I backed up, my feet wetted now by the shallow water, trying to face both of them. "Because you attacked. Drop your spears and leave me be," I said.

"You killed Massiaka there," the man said, faceless behind his mask of protective bronze. "We will not turn back now."

These were Paikans, practiced and deadly, in full armor. They were not the ragged rebels I'd bested this morning, which now seemed an eternity ago. These men wore armor and their spears gave them reach.

I'd killed their friend by surprise. They, on the other hand, would not die quickly.

I looked for some way to get out of this fight. "I was in the caravan. I did not ask to be attacked."

"It is too late," the Paikan on the right said.

My fingers loosened on the axe, getting ready for either man to attack me. The Paikans raised their spears, both of them out of reach of my axe, and they got ready to thrust them at me. But just as they stepped forward, crossbow bolts ripped out of the grass and smacked through their armor.

With grunts, they dropped to the pebble beach, armor crashing against the stone, spears clattering with them.

Five crossbowmen stepped out onto the pebbles. One of them was a short man with sweaty, raggedy hair limp over his forehead, dressed in a green robe. He slung the large wooden crossbow over his shoulder. "You are a brave woman, facing two Paikans on your own," he said with a laugh. "You may thank us for the favor we did you later."

I stared at the corpses.

"Three," I said to the man. I pointed to the dead one almost at his feet, and he pushed a torch in the body's direction to examine it.

"Well, well, well," he said.

"And you did me no damn favor," I continued. I didn't like the sound of 'thank me later.' I wanted to make sure they would think a little further before making assumptions about me. "The caravan still burns, the Paikans still ravage the land as they please. Nothing is changed."

The man looked thoughtful. "So you *are* from the caravan?"

"Yes." I still stood apart from them, hoping that they would move on without me. I had it in my head that I would start walking west in the hopes of getting to Paika, somehow.

Though, as Jal had said, it was hard to get into the city. Without the caravaner's help, I wasn't sure how I would do it, but I would have to think of something.

The man in the green robes looked back at me, then gestured at the bloodied axe. "There is more than one man's blood on there."

"More than one man attacked me back at the caravan."

He looked thoughtful. "Did you see how many war elephants charged?"

"I saw at least twelve from the Roadmaster's wagon," I said.

"Twelve!" said one of the other men. "I told you, we were sold bad information. They will rip through us like paper."

The green-robed man looked down at the stones. "We will need to recruit more men." His voice sounded bitter as he turned and looked out into the trees. "We will not try to take Paika this year, then."

"You're Jiva," I realized.

"I am Jiva," the man said. "My commanders here were about to go and scout the Paikan forces out there with our own eyes. We were hoping to avoid clashing with it until closer to Paika, but it seems they know we're out here."

One of the men behind Jiva spoke up. "What she says about the elephants is the same the other caravaners who escaped into the woods say. It's not worth the risk."

Jiva looked annoyed. "I know. I know. We'll return to camp."

"You have other caravaners at your camp?" I asked.

"A few survivors our scouts started finding in the woods," Jiva said. "That is what prompted us to come take a look."

I stared at him for a while, thinking about how to get to Paika. About the elephants. About what it would take to regain my children. Then I spoke without thinking. "If you are not going to use your army anytime soon, would you mind if I borrowed it to do what you wish to wait on?" I asked.

Jiva's commanders spluttered with laughter. But Jiva did not. His dark eyes narrowed, and anger surfaced. "Who are you to mock me?"

I rested my axe over my shoulder, hanging my arm over the shaft to balance it. "I am the Executioness."

One of the commanders stopped laughing. "You *do* exist!" he said.

Jiva glanced at him. "What idiocy are you talking about?"

"The refugees who came to us several weeks ago talk about an axe woman who faced forty Paikans on her own, defending Lesser Khaim from the Culling, until she fell from a sleeping spell they cast on her."

"Paikans don't use magic," Jiva said. "And if *she* is really the Executioness, she wasn't exactly killing them by the gross here, was she?"

I cleared my throat. "You interrupted me."

"Come with us and go back to your home, like the rest of us," Jiva said. "We will give you some water and food, what we can spare. The Alacaners will be excited to see you. Be glad you live."

"I am not glad I live," I shouted at him. "I do not share your cowardice! The Paikans stole my family from me. They burned my home to the ground. I have nothing left. Nothing but the hope of getting to Paika."

Jiva glowered. "I am here for the same reason. To fight back against the cullings. They took a daughter of mine, and I want my vengeance. But to call me a coward, well, it seems that you are eager to get yourself killed tonight."

"And you aren't?" I looked at the commanders around him. "The Paikans are looking for you, aren't they? My caravan was not the thing they came to destroy, was it? We were just a bonus. If you break apart to hide, it will be easier for them to take their time and seek out your parts."

Jiva's commanders looked at each other. "She is right. Once we split up, they can take their time to hunt us down one by one, like dogs."

"We have little in the way of supplies," Jiva said. "And, judging by the force that attacked your caravan, which is two hundred or so strong, with twelve war elephants you say, we are outmanned. Fighting men are in short supply throughout the lands, thanks to the culling. We don't have many horses for cavalry. The fight is over."

I shook my head. "The fight isn't over, you are just not able to see how best to bring it to them."

"You think you are a better commander than me?"

"No," I said. "I know nothing about armies or supply trains. But I do see the things that *men* do not."

Jiva, at first furious, now snapped his fingers. "Then, tell me what you see that I do not, woman, and I'll judge your words."

I had caught him, like a fish, and had his interest. "You think about their numbers, and whether you can compare yours to theirs, like two boys seeing who can piss the furthest."

As I had intended, the warlord jerked back from my words as if slapped. "Listen, axe-bitch…"

I spoke with a low voice, completely forcing him to stop in order to hear what I was saying. His commanders leaned forward. "The Paikans control the road. You can skulk in the woods like this, avoiding confrontation. Or you get an army so vast there is no hope for the Paikans at all."

"Since we have no vast army, but a couple hundred men, you think we should remain here, starving and hidden?" Jiva asked.

"No, starving accomplishes nothing," I said. "But with only two hundred men, you are not of much use. No, what I propose is you let me help you build an army so vast, so large, the Paikans will have no choice but to fold. They might not even choose to fight."

And, I thought, we would win the battle before even setting foot on the field.

Jiva folded his arms and laughed at me. "And where shall I find that army, Executioness? Shall I pull it out of my ass? Will you magic all the trees in this forest to suddenly take up my cause?"

I did not say anything, or change my expression, but waited, until one of the commanders repeated Jiva's question, "where will you find this army?"

"The lands are short of young men, due to the culling. But they are not short of angry, venomous mothers like me, whose families have been destroyed, and their towns scattered. And yet they live. They were the backbone of the caravan, before it was destroyed today. They haggle and trade in towns all up and down the coast. No doubt they even helped supply your army at times. There is your army, Jiva: an army of Executionesses, ready to throw themselves at the walls of Paika, like I am. No less thirsty for blood, no less able to be led into battle. No less able to kill when armed well."

Jiva unfolded his arms. "They will not fight as well as a man."

"Face me with your sword then, and find out how well a woman can fight," I said.

Jiva eyed my axe. Then he pointed at one of his commanders.

The man stepped forward, and his sword flashed out, faster than I had expected, but I shoved it aside with the axe clumsily.

On the second swing, I caught the blade in the curve of the axe's blade, and then spun the axe handle about to crack the man under the chin while his sword was still held away. I leapt back from his next slice, and smiled to see the blood and cracked teeth in his mouth.

He growled then, and began slashing quickly at me. I backed up further and further into the water as I kept the long blade away, almost tripping over my skirts in the mud that oozed under me.

We grunted, striking and clanging steel together. He was stronger, he was faster, and he would take me down.

But I refused him an easy kill.

By the end, we both stood in hip-deep water, panting, sizing each other up, when Jiva finally stood up from where he'd been squatting. "Good enough," he said. "Good enough. What will we arm this new army with?"

"Arquebuses where you can afford it," I said over my shoulder, still eyeing the commander before me. "Axes where you cannot."

"An arquebus is an expensive weapon for vain lords and the rich caravan. Do I look made of gold?" But I could hear in his voice that I had won. That he was taking me seriously.

"It took me a week to learn to shoot the arquebus. You'd have an army in that time."

"Anything else you want of me, besides what little fortune my army has amassed, then?"

With my axe still in front of me, I looked over at him. "Yes, I have another demand. We need a woman, called Anezka, from the caravan, if your scouts can find her among the survivors who are fleeing. She will be our link to getting us the supplies we need, and a new army."

Jiva clapped his hands. "It will be done, if she is alive and can be found. Now both of you, come in from the water, we need to return to camp and rest. Tomorrow we need to get further into the woods."

I held my axe in one hand, and held out my other to my opponent.

He spat a tooth out, and then grinned and took it.

Part Four

I T DID NOT HAPPEN as quickly as I wanted. But, it happened nonetheless.

First, with Anezka by my side, we recruited tallywomen from the remains of the caravan, and hagglers from the nearby villages. They melted off into the chill of the Northern forests with us, where the Paikans had to get off their horses and brave the bramble and tight brush.

Forges in half-destroyed towns built arquebus barrels, and woodsmen in the remains of once-great cities crafted stocks. Women all over began to carry axes, no matter where they went, or what hour of day it was.

And the Paikans did not know, for women taught other women how to fight with an axe or reload their arquebuses, and those women taught others. And what men paid close attention to what women did together?

Too few.

And those few that paid too much attention, found an axe buried in their skull.

Anezka's old caravan contacts kept food and supplies moving throughout old forest trails to us. Destroyed by the lack of trade and cullings, many were all too happy to help us in revenge for the caravan's destruction and antipathy to Paika. They even brought word of purges in Khaim, strange stories about the streets running with blood and the air above them glowing blue.

Jiva slunk into a gloom after the first months. "An army of widows," he complained. "We will be laughed at and destroyed."

"So take us on raids," I told him. "Kill anyone friendly to Paikans, burn their temples. But we will keep the women in hoods, so that we don't reveal ourselves just yet. You will see how strong they are in real battle."

Jiva resisted at first, but eventually took fifty women, armed with axes. Fifty men and fifty women fell upon one of the larger towns near Paika, overwhelming the thirty or so Paikans guarding the temples there. I watched the turrets of their temple topple into the flames with grim satisfaction, and then galloped with my sisters and brothers back into the protection of the northern forests.

And that was the last time Jiva spoke of weakness. His men stopped huddling off in the corner of the camp, feeling outnumbered. They passed among the women, and ate and joked with us.

"And now we have an army," Anezka muttered to me, when she saw that happen. I'd started to forget my previous life. My new life was weeks and weeks of drills, transporting the parts of arquebuses, and walking through dangerous forests.

"But do we have enough?"

"We have as many as we dare recruit. Any more, my supply routes fail, or we go broke. We have a month of supplies, money, and goodwill left," Anezka said.

She had a long scar on her cheek. Given to her when the caravan was destroyed.

It had been easy to recruit her. She'd gone from smiling caravaner to bloodthirsty soldier. Anything that would destroy Paika, or end with a Paikan's death, she enjoyed.

She carried a dagger now. Along with her axe and a heavy blunderbuss on her back carved with images of death and destruction along the stock and barrel. She even wore a silvered image of Tankan holding a spear around her neck, on a leather thong. It was not the halls of the merchantmen that Anezka hoped to spend eternity in, now, but the halls of a warrior god.

"Then I guess we're going to have to convince Jiva it's time to march," I said, and grabbed Anezka's forearm. "And that it's time to tear Paika down."

WE SWEPT south at first, and then westward. Jiva's men took the frontguard and fought any resistance. But there was little of that as we quickly advanced along the same spice road I'd travelled some six months ago. Just Paikan scouting parties, who usually galloped back up the road to take their reports to the city.

The road, I noticed, was more overgrown, more thick with bramble along the sides. But even that began to lessen. The woods and trees faded into hilly grasses and small farmsteads, recently abandoned.

We trudged like a normal army for the plains of Paika.

When we turned the last curve of the spice road, I gasped. The fields of Paika spread out before us, but they'd been emptied of what crops the laborers could harvest. Everyone

living there had moved back behind the protective walls of the city. Miles to the south, the sloping valley went out to the ocean, which was a distant glimmer. To the north were hills and mountains.

What a city it was!

The stone walls made a giant U before the mountain, and there were several smaller rings of walls higher up the slope of the city.

And then the rows and rows of streets and houses and windows and parapets that clung to the slope seemed to go on and on, only petering out when the hillside became so steep as to make building impossible.

Jiva laughed as he watched me from a horse that walked slowly along with us. "Do you think it still so possible to take the city?" he said.

"The battle was already won before we arrived," I said. Those walls would not fall easily, though.

"Maybe, maybe," Jiva said, and spurred his horse on.

"He's a bit excited," Anezka observed.

"A boy before battle," I replied.

We trickled through the empty farms and markets until we came to a stop on the edge of the fields just outside the thick walls.

An armored Paikan with a flag of negotiation flapping from a pole held in his saddle waited for us.

One of Jiva's commanders rode out to meet him.

When he came back, the commanders waved me over. Jiva threw a piece of parchment my way.

I looked down at it. I couldn't read: the words made no sense to a butcher from Lesser Khaim. So I looked back up at Jiva. "What is it?"

"The Hierarch of Paika wants to talk to you," Jiva said.

"Me?"

The bitterness on Jiva's face deepened. "I think he believes the Executioness to be the mind behind the army. The word has spread before us that the great Executioness marches with us. The lady who destroyed an entire Paikan army herself, after they razed Lesser Khaim."

I ignored the sarcasm in his voice. "I know nothing about tactics or negotiations," I said. "How can I speak for us?"

"Oh, but it does make sense," Jiva said. "That this army is yours as well as mine, there is a grain of truth to that. So go. Talk to their great leader, see what he demands or wants, then come back to us. If they keep you in there, have no fear, we will come soon after to rescue you."

I pulled Anezka over to me. "You have been in the city once before, will you come with me?"

She looked at the flag over the Paikan. "Will they honor the flag?"

"I can't promise it," I told her.

She mulled it over. "I'll come. I want to see their leader's face, I want to see if he realizes that he'll see his city taken by us."

I smiled at her. "We'll each have our victories soon, Anezka. Come."

We borrowed horses, and rode out across the field behind the Paikan negotiator toward the gates of Paika, where even more soldiers waited for us.

The steel doors shut once we were through, startling the horses with a loud rattle of chain as a giant weight fell down along the wall, the chains holding it yanking at pulleys and more chains that slammed the inch thick steel doors shut.

The Paikans led us through the cobbled streets, past fearful farmers camped with their livestock in what had once been markets, but were now shelters as they waited for the battles to begin.

We followed the Paikans up the steep, cramped streets, where we could hardly see the sky due to the two and three story buildings leaning in over us.

It reminded me slightly of Lesser Khaim, and I shivered as the horse's shoes echoed loudly around us.

At the top of Paika a final set of walls ringed an interior castle. Again, chains and weights rattled to shut the doors behind us.

The Hierarch of Paika waited for us by the battlements, the wind whipping at his robes.

"The Keeper of the Way, the enforcer of the Culling, and the ruler of Paika, the hierarch Ixilon, will speak with you," the negotiator told us, and waved his hand in a bow toward the hierarch.

From up here I could look out over the city, out into the fields where our armies gathered in loose clumps around the patchwork quilts of farmland and irrigation.

"I called you here to ask what it would take for you to surrender," Ixilon said.

I folded my arms. "You could have sent a message."

"I wanted you to see I was serious." Ixilon held his hands out. "And I wanted to see this legendary Executioness with my own eyes. I wanted to know what it would take to get you to stop this suicidal attack."

"You can give me back my children," I said simply. "Their names are Set and Duram. I have traveled from Khaim past Mimastiva, and all along the spice road on the coast to your lands. I survived the unprovoked attack on the great caravan by your people, and now I have finally arrived."

Ixilon looked down at the ground. "I did not know the names of your children. But I know that all the children from Khaim, where I was told you hailed from, have all left. They are on their way to the Southern Isles. They have chosen the Way. Their pilgrimage has begun. There is no calling them back until they are done. They have chosen the paths their lives will take them on."

"When did they leave?" I demanded.

"You will not catch them…"

"When?" I shouted at him.

The hierarch smiled. "If you were to leave now, on horseback, you might catch the last of the ships that are leaving."

I ran to the edge of the wall, looking at the roads down to the gates and out of the city. Anezka touched my arm. I turned and looked into her wide eyes.

"Will you go?" she asked me.

Would I go?

All I'd ever wanted was my family back. Could I have it by running for the harbor, far at the end of the valley? Or was it a trick?

Was it just a way for Ixilon to get me out of the way before the battle?

"You should surrender," I told Ixilon. "If you want to offer things, offer guarantees that families will no longer be pulled apart. That the cullings will stop. That you will reign peacefully over the coast. Then maybe we can discuss your future."

"I can only offer those things if you promise me that the bramble will cease appearing, or deliver me a way the bramble can be defeated," Ixilon said. "The Southern Isles my people hail from are small and carefully maintained. The sickness your people create from these lands floats to ours."

"You know I can't promise you the end of bramble. It cannot be destroyed, it can only be burned and hacked back," I snapped. "It is a curse we must all suffer."

"Then the culling must continue, and magic use must be checked," Ixilon said. "And we are at an impasse. Your people have to realize that there are consequences for your actions."

"Consequences? You speak of consequences," I spat at the raider. "Come stand at your walls here and look out at the consequences of your actions.

"Out there is an army that *you* have created."

Ixilon did look out. Then he looked back at me. "It is hardly an army. You want me to surrender by giving me a great show of numbers. But there are barely four hundred men out there. The rest of your army is made of women. Old maids. They call it the Widow's Army, and you've only had months to train them. I will plow through them, and my elephants will scatter your old women before us like dogs."

"Indeed," I said. "I've seen the remains of wars. And the men never seem to remember the women running from the sword who guided the army's packhorses to the frontline, and they always forget who bandaged the wounded through every skirmish. When the songs are sung about great battles, the women who helped sustain, feed, and build the army, who donated their husbands to the cause: they are always somehow forgotten. You forget that they are just as good at war as men. They fade in your memory only because they didn't share the glory of the front line, even though they often shared the losses and deaths.

"Now, these women at your walls: you've ripped their lives from them. They have nothing to live for but revenge. Their daughters, their sons, and their husbands are gone. Their farms are burned, their means of living are nothing but rubble. They are the walking dead, and are animated for one thing only, and that is revenge."

I walked over to Ixilon and stared into the calm eyes. "These women fear death little. Far less than the men you've paid to man these walls, or the ones who fight for some distant philosophy imported from your distant islands. Will your arrows stop the walking dead? Will your walls? Remember, this army welcomes death, because at least then it means they will find some sort of peace that has been taken from them! Can you fight an army created out of the pain of all who've lost their families Ixilon?"

I saw Ixilon's eyes flicker toward the battlements, a seed of doubt in there.

He walked over and grabbed the walls. His face looked pale, his eyes tired, and he suddenly seemed as if he'd shrunken in on himself.

"It is a challenge to my faith that we have achieved so little here on this coast," he said. "When we first came to Paika to spread the Way, we were attacked. After we took Paika, we built it up even greater so that we could protect our aftans and temples. And to defend ourselves, we trained larger and larger forces.

"You all were so resistant to the Way, and it was so much easier to teach to the orphans from your wars and collapsed cities, that soon it became easier to bring the collapse ourselves. It is often only in destruction that many can rebuild themselves. That is how it was with us."

Ixilon turned back, and I realized the man was shaken. "These cycles will never stop. We will always destroy ourselves."

"What in all the halls are you talking about?" I asked.

"He's talking about the Way," Anezka said. "Tell him to shut up, and let's leave."

But Ixilon ignored her. "The Five survivors found the Way. They were discovered on the Southmost Isle, forgotten, unable to build boats. The Five were all that remained of a whole island that had fought and killed itself, leaving the survivors to starve.

"My ancestors brought the Five back to the civilized isles. At first the Five grew fat and happy, and enjoyed the sweet breezes and palm shade. Until they observed war between the islands. They grew troubled, and were beset with visions of destruction and woe. They preached their visions on the streets together and starved themselves so that their ribs were like the hulls of half-finished ships.

"They were hung for inciting riots, but their martyrdom spread their message. Their visions of the future. And the Way spread: the understanding that the island of our world was all that there was. To reach out, to fight for things that could not be shared, would only bring us cannibalism, death, and the laughter of the gods."

Ixilon looked at me now. "So I have brought destruction and chaos, but only to prevent even worse. I want to save this world."

"By destroying it first," I said.

"We are a practical people," Ixilon said. "We are taught not to love things, to live austere lives and focus on productivity and wholeness. Some things that must be done are not inherently good. Even your people recognize this. It is like a parent spanking a child. Or like one of your leaders, who must use an executioner to kill magic users. We must pass the Way on, by any means, to your lands. It must be done."

"Then you are locked into your path, and I mine," I told him. "We are tools, forged by the ripples of what has been done, quenched in the blood of our actions."

"Come," Ixilon said, walking toward a turret door. "I have something to show you."

We followed him as he opened the door into a dim room. Two guards stood inside, and at a table, a large form sat in manacles by a bowl of fruits.

"Jal, is that you?" I moved closer, and he looked up.

He raised manacle-stained wrists to shield his eyes from the light. "Ah, the Executioness. I hear you are at the walls with an army, now. You've come far."

Ixilon stepped between us. "I could hand him back over to you. I could allow the caravan to run again."

"It's too late for that," I said. I wasn't going to suddenly change everything just because Ixilon had found Jal. He was no lover, or family member. Just an employer. An acquaintance. Ixilon had maybe thought I had been a caravaner, and that he was offering me a deal.

"I see that. Then I offer a mutual agreement. I will keep him here, safe for you," Ixilon said. "If you promise me something. Because I believe you're a person of your word."

I could hear the threat implicit. If I didn't agree, Jal would be killed. Ixilon seemed to think that would weigh heavy on me. Let him think it. I didn't care.

"What is it?" I asked.

"Do not kill the priests. Make them leave, but do not kill them. They teach the Way. They are not responsible for the culling. That lies on me, and the others who serve with me. The moral weight of the culling lies only with me and my soldiers. Would you agree?"

I looked back at Jal in the shadows of the room, then at Ixilon. "I will say yes. But only because I do not want to draw the judgment of Borzai for killing holy men, no matter what gods they serve. As we must all walk the halls of the gods someday."

Ixilon nodded. "I'm sorry we could not come to a peace."

"You forsook it the moment you rode with soldiers against children," I told him.

We left him still standing, looking out over his city.

Back in the fold of the army I rode to Jiva. "He has nothing for us," I told the warlord.

He looked up at the city and winced. He'd been hoping for a surrender. Somehow. But now he nodded and rode off to make preparations.

I raised up on the stirrups of the horse, and looked down the slope of the plains, off to the soft valley and the distant, sun glittered ocean.

Ixilon could have been lying that my children were there. It was definitely a distraction to get me away from the battle.

Yet, I would hate myself if I didn't try to see for myself.

I turned my horse's head to ride for the harbor.

But Anezka saw the move and grabbed my horse's reins. "You can't go," she said, firmly.

"My children might be getting on boats to leave," I said to her. "What would you have me do? It is the reason I came. Not to be in some great army. I came for them."

Anezka yanked on the reins to pull me alongside her. The horses huffed and sidled flank to flank. "If you leave, everyone will watch you flee for the valley. Many are here because they follow the Executioness. Your name, your reputation, has spread far and wide. If you leave, it will confuse their spirit."

"Their spirit? They are fighters. They are ready to avenge their families' deaths."

"Many of them will hear you're leaving to find your children, and run with you, hoping to find theirs," Anezka said.

I looked back at her. "As they should."

"No!" She grabbed my arm. "No. They shouldn't. Here we all stand, ready to end the Culling. Ready to stop the stealing of children, the destruction of our towns. You would throw away the chance to end all that for just your needs? You are the mother to all these fighters, you created them. You are the mother to a new generation of people who will not live under the thumb of the Paikans."

I slumped in the saddle. "I did not ask for all that. I am just Tana."

"You are not just Tana, you haven't been for months. And no one asks for the things that happen to them. You didn't ask for Lesser Khaim to be burned, any more than I asked for the caravan to be destroyed. But it has happened. And now you can stop it from all happening again."

I thought about Ixilon and his cycles of destruction, then straightened. I looked out beyond the mountain toward the slope of the land, where it carried on toward the coast, where Paikan ships would be leaving.

"I think you broke the last piece of me," I told Anezka.

"You and I were already broken," she said, and then she led me deeper into the camp, her arm still holding mine.

THE SUN was orange and fat over the plains in its midmorning bloat when the Paikans burst from their clanking gates. War elephants roared, the sound racing out across the fields to us as we formed up.

"He should hold behind his walls," Anezka said as twenty elephants moved out onto the field, followed by a hundred Paikans on horseback. Four hundred soldiers followed the riders, each in a square group of fifty, those long spears bristling like ship's masts from each person. We could see lines of archers up on the walls, tiny faces looking back at us. "It would take us a year to breach them."

"Ixilon knows he will eventually need to fight," I told her. "That's what Jiva says. Better to do it upfront when the men are healthy and not starving, when they still believe they are invincible and eager, instead of demoralized."

We stood on foot in a cluster of eight hundred women in the field, the ones who were all armed with both arquebuses and axes. "He still thinks one of his men is better than four of us," Anezka noted, looking at the numbers.

Two thousand total armed women had come to the field. Those not in my square of eight hundred with arquebuses carried just simple axes. Jiva's men were on their horses and ready to break for the gates from the side, preventing Ixilon from retreating back into the city.

"We'll soon find out," I said to Anezka. "I'm just grateful he's keeping his archers on the walls where they can't reach us just yet."

The ground shook as the war elephants began their charge. I turned back around to look at my own army. They shifted, nervous at the sight of the armored elephants thundering toward them.

Someone raised an arquebus, and Anezka spotted the movement and screamed, "keep your weapons pointed down, do not fire until the order flags go up!"

But I understood the impulse.

There were five lines of women, our most untrained recruits, that we stood with. It was quickest to teach them how to aim and shoot the arquebus. They had all been the last to join.

And breaking the Paikans depended on them more than the axe fighters.

The elephants loomed larger, their armor clanking, the ground shaking. Paikans followed behind, the charge moving quicker as they closed.

I could see the closest elephant's eyes now. The wrinkles in its long trunk that slapped back and forth as it ran.

The order flags whipped into the air, something Anezka had copied from the caravan to simplify ordering our untrained army around, and the first row of a hundred women raised their arquebuses. The entire row of newly hammered metal tubes gleamed. Slow burning fuses sparked down the line as they were lit.

The second row, the moment the first row raised, also began preparing to fire.

An elephant screamed rage, and in answer, the first line of arquebuses answered. The thunder of fire matched the earthquake of giant's hooves. Smoke rose and filled, and then came the second line of thunder.

Shrieks of inhuman pain pierced the smoke, and the first of the elephants stumbled through the powder haze, crashing into the first line and tumbling to the ground. Then another stumbled through.

Women dropped their arquebuses, and though untrained with their axes, fell upon the elephants like they were firewood, hacking both their riders and the beasts as they writhed and screamed on the ground.

"We told them to leave the elephants once they fell," I snapped, frustrated.

"They're caught up in it all," Anezka said. "There are lines behind them. It is not a problem yet."

Some were reloading though, even as the square formations of Paikans bristling long spears came quickly through the curtain of smoke. But they were expecting to find us scattered.

Instead, they met three more rows of thunder, and then scattered pops from those in the remains of the first and second lines who had managed to reload their arquebuses.

Paikans stumbled and fell, and the impenetrable wall of spears faltered.

The axe women came from deep behind the lines and ran at the corners of the Paikan formations. They hit the spears in a bloody mangle of bodies and blades. The squares deformed, split down their centers as the fighting degenerated into one-on-one combat.

I still stood in the second line, no more than a hundred feet away from the stalled spearmen and fighting. A wounded elephant groaned just fifty feet off to my right, a large grey hill that prevented me from seeing Paika.

I moved forward with Anezka, bringing my arquebus up once to sight on a raider that charged us and firing.

He dropped, and we stepped over him to climb the dying elephant and gain a better view of the hell that we had helped design.

The clumped Paikans were slowly being overwhelmed all around me, but the well-armored soldiers on horses still milled about the gates of Paika.

I raised my axe into the air and pointed at Paika, and saw the faces of hundreds of women finish reloading their guns to look at me.

"Paika!" I screamed and waved the axe. We had stalled their spears, broken them apart, now I wanted us to run through the open field and into the city. "Paika!"

"Paika!" they screamed back.

As I crawled down from the elephant I could hear the sound of Jiva's horsemen moving now, moving full tilt towards the raider horsemen.

They galloped ahead of us, their way clear, and we ran after them.

Horse crashed into horse and the screams of the dying began. With the horsemen countered, the horde behind me swept through the Paikans as a rain of whispering arrows struck the ground all around us.

Then we poured into the city itself, arquebuses firing. We threw the long, ungainly weapons aside for axes as we met archers, and a few Paikan soldiers who had been left inside. And my words to Ixilon came true, as the axe-wielding women threw themselves with grim revenge against any armed Paikan they encountered.

I ran up the streets, gasping for breath and dizzy from exertion, almost ready to pass out by the time we reached the last battlements.

Anezka had run up the hills well ahead of me.

"They never even had time to close the gate," she said.

"Then we've won!" I hadn't even bloodied my axe, and it was over. We had torn the Paikans down. "We've done it."

From up here, as I looked around, I could see smoke beginning to billow up from the city. And the field was empty of living soldiers. Only the dead and injured, lying in the mud made by our feet, lay out there like small dolls or figures in a painting regarded from a distance.

When I looked back at Anezka I did not see the same happiness. "There's something you should see," she said.

She took me into that turret I'd been in the day before, and my mouth dried even before the door opened and I looked inside.

An ashen-faced Ixilon looked back up at me, then quickly down at the table he sat at, his wrists bound with rope. Behind him, Jal slumped, a long spear run through the whole of his chest stuck out of both sides of the man.

"You killed him anyway?" I asked.

Ixilon licked his lips, and did not look up at me. "A guard, not me."

A badly beaten guard in the corner of the room croaked, "Payback, for the whore who dared take the city."

The fury that lived inside me exploded. I grabbed my axe and crossed to where Ixilon lay with his head in his hands, and swung the axe deep, easily, and precisely toward the back of his neck.

I swerved at the last second, and buried it into the wood of the table just short of his ear.

"You failed," I told Ixilon. "You failed as a man to keep just a simple promise to me, and you failed in your attempt to foist your Way upon this land: there will be no more cullings now. And the land will be better for it."

I had done my duty for all the other mothers in these lands. But now it was time to do something I'd yearned to do since I'd met Ixilon. I ran from the room and into Anezka. "Get me a horse. Now!"

"Please, listen to me first. Jiva's dead, you need to talk to the commanders," she said. "They need to hear from you…"

"A damned horse! Now!" I shoved past her and ran down the cobblestones with a tired limp until I saw a horseman. "Give me your horse," I demanded.

"Who are you to…" he started to say, but then he saw the axe, and my face, and realized who I was, and slid off.

"Tana!" Anezka called.

"You are as much one of this army's leaders as I am," I shouted at her. "You take care of it. In my name if you must. But you take care of it."

I galloped off as fast as the horse could manage down the hill, around the curves, and then out the gates. I pushed the horse as hard as I dared, until foam flecked its mouth and it ignored my demands.

Getting down from the horse I stumbled along the empty roads of the small town that had sprung up to serve the Paikan harbor.

Eyes looked at me from behind shuttered windows.

I staggered out to the end of one of the piers and looked out at the gray sea, and in the far distance, watched a single sail slowly disappear over the edge of the ocean, headed South.

It was doubtful my sons were on that last boat. But standing there, it felt like it.

They had left me and moved on.

I crumpled to the wooden planks. I could not find tears, but my body shook as if I were trying to remember how to cry.

Anezka found me still on the edge of the pier hours later.

She said nothing, but waited at the start of the stones of the waterfront until I decided myself to turn my back to the ocean.

"What are you doing here?" I asked her.

"It was truly as much your army as it was Jiva's," she said. "We've won. And now we need to plan what comes next."

I let myself get recaptured by her, and returned to the city.

I THINK of philosophers as drug-addled dreamers who see only the reflections cast on their blackboards. The shadows of the world as it really exists around them. They say there is no such thing as good and evil. They talk about choice and flux, intersections and perspectives and situations.

They may well be correct. Who am I, an old peasant mother, to question those who spend their lives poring over these questions? And since I decree it, any philosopher or religion that forsakes weapons at my city's gate can come to Paika. My city. And they do so flock, like hungry sheep, to my markets.

I did this for my sons, against counsel, so that they would have a city on the coast to return to if they choose. They follow the Way, now, and I cannot bring myself to chase those who follow the same beliefs as my sons from these coasts.

I will be here, when they get back from the Southern Isles. I will be here for them, even if we might hardly recognize each other.

The thinkers say it is the way of the world for things to change. That includes people, I gather.

So even though we grow unrecognizable to each other I am still their mother, and this is still their land.

I hold back the bramble as best I know how. At first, I did not care to hunt people in the city. But those who did not follow the Way, my own people, began using magic, and bramble began to choke our streets.

I fought the Paikans to get my children back. To stop the culling. I had no wish to return to forcing the Way on people. And so I am forced to find the magic users, as I must, and hang them from the city's walls. On my worst days, I think I have become no better than the Jolly Mayor. And to my chagrin, the Way's priests point to the people I execute as proof that only the Way can save these lands.

I do all these things because even though I am a mother, I am also now a new person. I am the queen of Paika, the lady of the lands in its shadow.

I am the Executioness.

And I am waiting for my children to come home.